THE JOURNEY THAT NEVER ENDS

NEVER ENDS

TINY HOMES AND HAPPY TAILS SERIES

JODI ALLEN BRICE

To everyone who thinks it's too late to start over.
Trust me.
It's not.

CHAPTER 1

*E*lana Taylor pressed a hand to her stomach before stepping into her parent's' palatial home in the gated subdivision of Charleston, South Carolina. Despite being a thirty-year-old woman, she dreaded being summoned home and feeling like an incompetent child again. Whatever the reason for this family meeting, it wouldn't be good. The last family meeting had resulted in more charitable duties being assigned to her and her two younger sisters, Elizabeth and Brianna. While her sisters loved being in the spotlight where they could showcase their magnanimous deeds, Elana preferred to work behind the scenes, away from the watchful eyes of the public. Being the center of attention was not her thing. Besides, it was already hard to balance her own fledgling career with her charitable commitments. Elana glanced down at her black jeans and cream-colored shirt. There hadn't been time to go home and change since her father's call had sounded dire.

Elana took a steadying breath and made her way to the library, which doubled as her father's office. The ballet-style flats didn't make a noise on the hardwood floors. The elaborate artwork on the walls seemed to look down on her. Home was supposed to be inviting, not feel like a cage. Elana stepped inside the stately double doors of the library. Her father, John Taylor, glanced up from behind his colossal mahogany desk and stood.

"Hello, Father." Elana forced a smile.

He dropped the paper he was holding and furrowed his brows. "Elana. You're late."

Shifting her weight, she dropped the smile. "Sorry. I was finishing up a project at work. It's an ad campaign for the library."

Her mother, Victoria, stepped into the room dressed in a pristine blue suit. "I thought that project was due two days ago?"

Elana bit the inside of her cheek. "They granted me an extension."

Her father sighed and walked around the desk to place a kiss on her forehead. "Dear, you must manage your time better. You know what I always say…"

Elana nodded. "It's always better to be early than late. And that applies to deadlines and dinner."

He smirked, pleased that she had remembered his sage words.

She lifted her chin. "I see that Elizabeth and Brianna aren't on time either." She'd never been close to her younger sisters. Her mother was always pitting her against them.

The echo of high heels resonating off the hardwood floors had her turning around.

Brianna and Elizabeth both grinned. One was carrying a tray with scones, while the other held a tray with a pot of hot tea, and teacups and saucers. They wore designer dresses and their blonde hair was perfectly fixed. Unlike Elana's.

"We're not late. We've been here at least an hour, waiting on you, silly." Brianna smirked.

Elana bristled and felt her face heat with embarrassment. She hated being reminded that she wasn't as organized as her siblings were. She smoothed down her blouse and focused on her father. "So, what's this meeting about?"

Her mother turned and gave her a sweet smile. "It's about Grandma Cecilia."

Elana's eyes went wide. "Is she okay? Did something happen?"

Her father scanned her mother's face before looking at her. "Physically, she is fine. But mentally, well, she's not as sharp as she once was. Just yesterday, she put her keys in the refrigerator. Who knows what she'll do next? She might forget and leave the stove on and burn her house down."

Elana studied her father. "She has Anna, the housekeeper. She has always taken great care of Grandma Cecilia and won't let her burn the house down."

Her father studied her. "Not anymore. I fired Anna today. Mother won't need her anymore."

Elana was at a loss for words. When she found them, she blurted them out. "You what? Why would you fire Anna?"

Her mother walked over and patted her hand. "We won't need Anna anymore, sweetheart," her mother said. "Grandma Cecilia is going to an assisted living facility. I'm sure she'll be happy there around so many people her age."

Elana couldn't believe what she was hearing. "You're putting Grandma Cecilia in a nursing home?"

Elizabeth rolled her eyes. "Not a nursing home. It's assisted living. It's like a resort for old people."

Elana glared at her younger sister. "I can't believe Grandma Cecilia agreed to this."

Her mother poured a cup of tea into the exquisite china cup and handed it to Elana. "That's where you come in, dear."

Elana swallowed hard and gazed around the room. She

got the uneasy feeling she was being used for something sinister.

Elizabeth grinned at her. "Grandma Cecilia appreciates your opinion."

Elana studied her beautiful younger sister, who always had it together. At age twenty-four, Elizabeth had started her own decorating company and was doing well. Even twenty-two-year-old Brianna had gotten her real estate license and was making money hand over fist. Elana was still driving the car she'd gotten when she graduated high school and had only gotten one raise since she'd started working at the advertising agency. She'd always suspected her parents had decided to have more children when they'd figured out Elana would not be as successful as they'd hoped.

"What are you talking about?" Elana sighed.

Her father gave her a stern look. "We want you to go over to Grandma's and talk her into going into an assisted living facility. She'll take it better if you address it." He walked around the desk and handed her some formal documents. "You also need to talk her into signing these papers."

She examined the papers and then looked up at him. "This document gives you power of attorney over all her finances."

He nodded and sat back down in his chair. "She needs someone responsible to watch over her money. For the past few months, she has been sending big amounts to someone online. I fear her judgment is slipping."

Brianna stood up and scowled. "She's going to give all her money away, and there won't be any inheritance for us." She crossed her arms over her chest, looking very much like an impudent child.

Elana eased into a nearby chair. "I don't know. I didn't get the idea that her judgment was impaired the last time I saw her. I'm sure there is a reasonable answer to all of this."

Elizabeth snorted. "I think she's getting catfished."

Her mother handed her father a cup of tea. "Catfished? What is that?" She gave her daughter a baffled look.

"Catfishing is where someone pretends to be a different person online than they are in real life. The goal is to make the victim fall in love with the catfish. Once they have their trust, they talk them into sending them money."

Her mother pressed a polished hand to her chest. "Oh my. That sounds serious."

Her father stared at Elana. "Which is why we need to get a power of attorney to stop her from sending all her money to a stranger. Do you understand the seriousness of this now?"

Elana nodded and took a sip of her tea. The liquid turned bitter in her stomach. "I'll go over today and talk to her."

Her father beamed. "Good girl. I knew I could count on you."

The idea of having to tell Grandma Cecilia she needed to give up her independence was almost more than she could bear.

Setting her tea down, she gathered her purse. "I think I'll go over to her house now. The sooner this conversation is over, the better."

CHAPTER 2

*E*lana hated to be the one to talk to her grandmother about the assisted living. She wished there was another way, but if what her parents were saying was true, Grandma Cecilia needed to be protected.

Her heart ached as she turned into the circular driveway of her grandmother's home. She parked and got out of her car.

Unlike her parents' mansion, her grandmother's home was modest. It was the same home she and her late husband had bought years ago when they were just starting out. Grandma Cecilia once told her she did not need to impress someone with a new house. She liked her house just fine and didn't care what anyone else thought.

Grandma Cecilia had been widowed for over thirty-two years. Her grandfather had died of a massive heart attack before Elana was born.

Her father had told her that after his father had died, Grandma Cecilia had thrown her time and attention into her fledging business of fishing lures, tackle, and equipment. She turned it into a multimillion-dollar venture over the years.

Grandma Cecilia was as astute a businesswoman as Elana had ever seen.

Elana studied the house. She wondered... if Grandma Cecilia moved into assisted living, would the house be sold?

Walking up to the door, Elana blinked back the sting of tears.

She pressed her finger to the doorbell and waited while the sounds spilled through the house.

Anna flung open the door, and she looked relieved.

"Elana, it's you. I thought it might be..."

Elana cocked her head. "My father?"

Anna nodded nervously. "Yes." She stepped back to let her in. "Please come in."

Anna had been with Grandma Cecilia for the past twenty years. She was the same age as Elana's mother, but you would never know. Anna didn't try to color her gray hair nor did she visit the plastic surgeon yearly like her mother did. Anna might appear her actual age, but Elana thought her more beautiful than her mother.

Anna had originally worked for Grandma Cecilia as a housekeeper, keeping the house tidy. As Grandma Cecilia got older, Anna took on more responsibility, like taking her grandmother to her doctor appointments and making her meals.

Elana gave Anna a hug. "How's she doing?"

Anna's brow furrowed. "Physically? Strong as an ox. But she is getting forgetful."

Elana swallowed. "I heard about the keys in the fridge."

Anna gave her a worried look. "That's what I told your father."

Elana blinked. "Did something else happen?"

Anna bit her lip. "She let Winston out in the backyard to potty last night. When he didn't come back within a few minutes, she went outside to retrieve him. She comes walking through the door. She's holding something, but it's not Winston. It was a raccoon. I have no idea how she caught it, but the dang thing nearly bit my hand when I tried to take it from her."

Elana gaped. "Is she okay?"

Anna nodded. "She's fine. I made her throw the raccoon out the door, and then I found Winston." She sighed heavily. "Come on into the kitchen and I'll make some tea."

Elana put her hand on the woman's arm. "I'm afraid I'm not here to socialize. My father sent me."

Anna nodded slowly. "He wants to put your grandmother in a nursing home. He told me that after he gave me my six-week notice."

Elana shifted her weight and swallowed the lump of emotion rising in the back of her throat. "It's assisted living. Not a nursing home."

Anna shook her head vehemently. "I don't care what you call it. It's not right. Cecilia needs someone to stay with her overnight permanently. I would, but since my daughter, Gail, had her baby, I must help her at night."

Elana nodded. Gail's husband Marcus was in the military and stationed overseas. "How much longer is Marcus's military tour?"

Anna's brows furrowed. "Four more months until he can come home. I can't image how hard it's been on Gail. Having a baby while her husband is always deployed."

Elana reached over and squeezed her hand. "It won't be that much longer. Gail is lucky to have a mother like you to help her."

Anna gave her a grateful smile. "That's kind of you to say, Elana. Come on. I'll take you to Cecilia."

Elana followed the woman into the living room. Every available inch of space held a plant. When Grandma Cecilia wasn't digging around in her garden, she was tending to her houseplants.

Anna opened the back door and called out. "Cecilia. Elana is here to see you."

Grandma Cecilia's head popped up from the flower bed. She gave a wave and got to her feet.

Anna turned back to Elana. "I'll bring you both some tea."

Elana forced a smile before Anna headed into the kitchen. She wasn't in the mood for tea, but she didn't want to be rude to Anna.

"Elana! What a wonderful surprise!" Grandma Cecilia walked in the back door. She gave Elana a warm hug.

"Hi, Grandma." Elana pulled back and studied the older woman's face for any signs of change. It had been about three weeks since she last saw her.

Her white hair was windblown from being outside, but other than a few more wrinkles around her eyes, she looked the same.

"Come sit. I'm worn out from planting."

Elana frowned. "But it's fall. What are you planting that will bloom this late in the season?"

Grandma Cecilia barked out a laugh. "It's tulip bulbs. And you plant them now so they will bloom in the spring."

Elana laughed. "So much for my gardening skills. I'm not a master gardener like you."

Grandma brightened when Anna walked into the room with a tray holding a pot of tea and teacups. "Ah, Anna. Thank you, dear."

Anna poured them each a cup before heading out of the room to give them some privacy.

Grandma Cecilia sat in one of the floral wingback chairs and sipped her tea. "I suppose you are here to talk me into going to a nursing home."

Elana nearly choked on her tea. She set the teacup down

on the side table and looked at her grandmother. "Did Dad tell you?"

Her grandmother barked out a laugh. "Absolutely not. He doesn't want the cat out of the bag so quickly. I eavesdropped on the landline when he was giving Anna her notice." She narrowed her eyes. "I'm not crazy."

Elana bobbed her head. "I know that, Grandma. I'm here to find out your side of the story."

She lifted her chin. "I'm going to tell you something, and I don't want you to tell your father or anyone else."

Elana frowned. "Okay."

Grandma Cecilia studied her. "Promise me."

Elana sighed. "I promise."

A slow smile grew on her grandmother's thin lips. "I have someone that I've been talking to. Someone special."

Elana's stomach sank. Those were not the words she wanted to hear from her grandmother.

"We've been talking online." She giggled.

"Grandma, sometimes people pretend to be someone they are not. Talking to someone online without seeing them is dangerous." She clasped her hands in her lap.

Grandma Cecilia snorted. "I know him better than my family. He truly loves me."

Elana shifted in her seat. She didn't like the way this conversation was going.

"Grandma, have you been sending this person money?"

Her grandmother gave her a surprised look. "Why, yes. How did you know?"

Elana cleared her throat.

Suddenly, Grandma Cecilia stood from her chair. "Your father. Your father has been looking into my personal account." She fisted her hands at her side. "The nerve!"

Elana stood and gently squeezed her grandmother's arm. "He only wants to protect you."

Grandma Cecilia glared at her. "Get your head out of the clouds, Elana. Your father wants control of my money."

Elana swallowed back the lump in her throat. She hated confrontation. Avoided it at all costs. That's why she preferred to stay out of family business.

Her grandmother cocked her head and studied her. "I tell you what. You come with me on a road trip to see my true love. If we arrive there and he's not who he says he is, then I'll sign power of attorney over to your father. And I'll go to the nursing home without raising a ruckus."

Elana narrowed her eyes. "It's assisted living."

Grandma Cecilia shrugged. "Same thing. So, what do you say? Feel up for a road trip?"

She worried her lip with her teeth. "What's the catch?"

Grandma Cecilia snorted. "The only catch is it must be a road trip. In my old VW van."

Elana's shoulders sank. "Grandma, that thing is old as dirt. I don't think it's going to get us where we need to go without breaking down on the side of the road."

Grandma let out a roll of laughter. "Of course it will. I have my retired neighbor come over once a month to crank it up and check all the fluids. She is solid. It will get us where we need to go." She beamed.

Elana didn't really see a downside. She stuck out her hand. "Deal. Now, do you mind telling me where we are going?"

A sneaky smile stretched across the woman's weathered face. "Montana."

CHAPTER 3

*A*fter leaving her grandmother's house, she called her father and filled him in on the entire conversation.

"I really don't know that I can take that much time off from work. I shouldn't have agreed to drive her, but she seemed so determined." Elana took a left on her way home.

"Actually, I think it's a great idea." Her father sounded pleased.

"You do?" Elana slammed on her brakes to keep from hitting a crazy driver who was weaving in and out of traffic. Sometimes she entertained the idea of living in a small town where the pace was much slower.

"Yes, I do. Once you get her to Montana and she realizes what a fool she has been, she'll agree that she needs help to manage her finances. And don't worry about your job. I'll call Mark and work everything out for you."

Elana cringed. "You don't have to do that. I can call him myself." She wasn't a child anymore. She could take her of her own business.

"Whatever you want. And Elana, I just want to say how

proud I am of you. I knew you were the right person for the job." He ended the call.

Her gut tightened. Why did this feel so bad for Grandma Cecilia?

The second she pulled into her driveway by her one-bedroom cottage in the older part of town, her phone buzzed with a text.

She glanced down. It was from Anna.

Your grandmother sent a list of clothes you'll need to get for the road trip. She says you guys are leaving at six a.m. sharp, so don't be late. Plan to be gone for almost three weeks ~ Anna.

She groaned. "I don't need new clothes. I have clothes." Grabbing her purse, she headed inside.

When she stepped inside her cozy little home, she breathed a little easier.

She dumped her keys and purse on the table in the small foyer and went into her bedroom.

Kicking off her shoes, she opened her closet and pulled out the largest suitcase she had. She would have to stuff three weeks' worth of clothes in one bag.

She pulled out a pair of sneakers, some black flats, and one pair of heels. She'd wear the sneakers while driving and the flats and heels whenever they went out to eat.

After packing the rest of her clothes, which included a lot of jeans and T-shirts, along with a few pairs of slacks and blouses, she glanced up at the top of the closet at the big floppy hat she always wore to the beach. It might come in handy if they stopped along the way to do some sightseeing. Standing up, she grabbed the hat and tossed it on top of her suitcase.

Packing done, she headed into the kitchen to fix something for dinner.

Elana opened the refrigerator and pulled out some left-over pasta salad from the night before. There wasn't much left, so she didn't bother getting a plate. Instead, she grabbed a fork and ate right out of the plastic container.

Turning on her laptop, she sat at the tiny kitchen table she'd thrifted. She typed in how far it was from South Carolina to Montana. Her fork froze halfway to her mouth when she saw the results.

"Holy cow. It's going to take a week of driving just to get there," she muttered to herself. Grabbing her phone, she put in the directions.

It was going to be a long trip. She wasn't sure if Grandma Cecilia understood just how long.

Maybe her grandmother would see how baffling this road trip was and get Elana to turn around.

Closing the laptop, she went over to the sink and rinsed out her container before sticking it in the dishwasher.

She glanced out the window into the backyard. It was dark, and morning would come way too soon.

Elana padded into her bedroom to get ready for bed and the adventure that she'd somehow found herself in.

CHAPTER 4

$\mathcal{E}$lana looked on in horror as Grandma Cecilia went through her packed suitcase to pare it down.

"Elana, you don't need this many pairs of pants, and you won't be needing any of these nice clothes. Jeans and T-shirts only. And you didn't even pack a coat."

Elana shook her head. "It's ninety degrees."

Her grandmother smirked. "It's ninety degrees here. But once we hit the mountains, the temps drop drastically. I have an extra coat you can wear." Grandma Cecilia stood and looked at her. "And you can't take a suitcase. There won't be enough room." She shoved a plastic trash bag into Elana's arms. "Put your clothes in here."

Elana frowned but didn't argue. Instead, she knelt in front of the meager clothes she could take and shoved them in the bag.

Grandma Cecilia glanced at her watch. "We're behind schedule. We need to get on the other side of Atlanta today. I have a meeting in Mississippi tomorrow." She opened the doors to the VW van and put her bag of clothes on the bench seat and a bag of what appeared to be snacks on the floor.

Elana shook her head. "We're not going through Mississippi. That's out of our way."

Grandma Cecilia poked her head out of the van and motioned for Elana to hand her the bag of clothes. "I don't care that it's out of our way. This is a road trip, Elana. You go with the flow. Besides, I have to meet someone in Mississippi."

Elana sighed. Grandma Cecilia gave her a look.

"So, who are you meeting with in Mississippi? An old friend?"

Grandma Cecilia stepped out of the van and shut the door before grabbing her sunglasses and shoving them over her eyes. "No. A new friend." She opened the passenger door and clambered inside.

Elana cut her eyes at Anna, who was standing in the driveway to see them off. "Are you going to be okay?"

Anna smiled and nodded. "Of course. I'll come by every day and check on the house. I packed a small cooler of sandwiches and fruit. It's in the back. Call and give me an update when you can."

Anna pulled Elana into a hug, and Elana squeezed her tight. "I will. Thanks for everything, Anna."

She walked around to the driver's side and climbed in.

Her grandmother dangled the keys in front of her. "Ready for an adventure?"

Elana snorted. "One's person's adventure is another person's ordeal."

Grandma Cecilia roared with laughter.

After seven hours of driving—plus ten bathroom breaks—they rolled into Atlanta.

"Which hotel do you want to stay in? Marriott or Hilton?" Traffic was at a standstill, and Elana was trying to search for places to stay on her phone.

"We are staying here. I already made reservations." Grandma Cecilia shoved her cell phone in Elana's direction.

Elana couldn't find the name of the hotel but started following directions on Grandma Cecilia's phone once the traffic started moving.

Thirty minutes later, they passed the city limits.

"I don't think this is right," Elana said. "There are no hotels out in this direction."

Grandma shook her head. "We're not staying at a hotel. We are staying here." She pointed out the windshield.

Elana groaned when she saw an RV park out in the middle of nowhere.

CHAPTER 5

$\mathcal{E}$lana pulled up to the office of the RV park and glanced over at her grandmother. "Did you book a cabin?" She'd noticed the tiny wood structures when they came through the entrance.

Her grandmother snorted and handed her a sheet with the confirmation. "Here, just give them this. They'll tell you where to go. It's already paid for, so don't let them try to upsell you for bigger accommodations."

Elana took the confirmation of their reservation and slid out of the car. She stood and stretched her arms over her head. She couldn't wait to get a hot shower and something to eat, then fall into bed.

As Elana opened the door to the office, an older woman wearing a bright-yellow shirt standing behind the counter greeted her. "Welcome!"

Elana smiled. "Hi. We have reservations for tonight." She gave the woman the piece of paper with the confirmation details.

"Perfect." The woman smiled and entered some information into the computer. She grabbed a map of the RV park and drew a line with a pink highlighter. "Here is where we are, and if you follow this line"—she tapped the paper—"here is your spot. The showers are open 24 hours, and here's the code to enter." She scribbled four numbers on the map and handed her two towels and washcloths.

Elana frowned. "The cabins don't have showers?"

The woman frowned. "No. just beds."

Elana felt her shoulders slump.

"Do you have any more questions?"

Elana shook her head. "No, thank you." She grabbed the map and headed back to the van.

Her grandmother brightened when she got back to the vehicle. "Everything set?"

Elana cringed. "The cabins don't have showers. We have to use the public showers." She shoved the map and the towels at her grandmother. "The code is at the bottom of the map."

Grandma Cecilia grinned. "I feel like a girl at summer camp. What about you, Elana?"

Elana arched a brow. "I never went to summer camp, so I wouldn't know."

She started the van and followed the directions on the map to where they'd be spending the night.

Elana frowned when she drove up to spot 23. "This can't be right. This is a camping pad. It's not a cabin."

Her grandmother shook her head. "I didn't reserve a cabin. I reserved this pad. So back in and let's get out."

Elana whipped her head around to face her grandmother. "Wait. You did what? Why would you get an RV pad? We have nowhere to sleep."

Grandma Cecilia beamed. "Yes, we do. One person can sleep in the van while the other sleeps in a tent. I made sure that Anna packed the tent supplies in the very back."

Elana blinked. She couldn't believe her ears. "You

mean..." Before she could say any more, someone honked behind her.

"Come on, dear. Back this van in so we aren't blocking the road." Her grandmother patted her hand.

Elana pulled forward a bit before putting the van in reverse and backing into the spot they had reserved for the night.

"Perfect. Now let's get out and fix something for dinner." Grandma Cecilia clambered out and shut the door behind her.

Elana slammed her mouth shut. She knew her grandmother would not enjoy camping out and would finally relent and get a hotel for tomorrow night. Maybe a cute bed-and-breakfast in that small town of Harland Creek that they were supposed to stop at. After killing the engine, Elana grabbed the keys and got out of the van.

Grandma Cecilia wiped her hand across the metal picnic table and grimaced. "Elana, grab those wipes out of the van. This table needs to be cleaned."

Elana hiked her purse on her shoulder and opened the side door of the van and climbed inside.

She found the wipes underneath the tiny sink and pulled them out. She handed the container to her grandmother.

Her stomach rumbled.

"Let's start dinner. I think Anna packed some hot dogs in the cooler. And there are some chips and buns as well." Grandma Cecilia didn't waste any time but started wiping down the metal picnic table.

Elana found the hotdogs and the bag of food and plopped them down on the table.

"We need to make a fire to get these cooked. There's enough leftover wood in the firepit, and I saw some matches in the glove box."

Elana nodded. "I'll get them." She returned with matches

in hand to see Grandma Cecilia stacking the wood together. Elana bent and stuck a match. It lit on the first strike, and she held it to the wood, but it didn't catch fire.

"We need something like kindling. Paper, maybe?"

A balding man in a pop-up camper parked beside them was busy getting something out of the back of his truck. He gave them a wave and a smile. "Sorry to eavesdrop, but you ladies need lint if you want to start a fire."

Grandma Cecilia frowned. "Lint? From a dryer?"

He bobbed his head. "Yes. It's the perfect thing to get a fire started." He pulled a plastic Ziplock bag out of his back pocket and handed it to them. "Here you go."

Elana frowned. "You don't need it?"

He shook his head. "I get some every time I dry my clothes. Besides, I am heading out in the morning, so I won't need it."

Elana took it. "Thank you."

He smiled. "Of course. I love sharing tips on outdoor living. You ladies have a good evening." He gave them a smile and headed back to his camper.

"That was nice of him." Elana stared at the pile of lint in the plastic bag.

Grandma Cecilia looked up at her. "Outdoorsy people usually are. The more time you spend outside, the more likely you are to have a friendly attitude. It's because of the vitamin D." She pointed to the firepit. "Now let's try out his trick for starting a fire."

Elana bent down and grabbed another match. She opened the bag and pulled out a wad of lint and positioned it under the small stack of wood. When she lit the match, she held it to the lint.

It immediately caught fire, and she fed some smaller twigs under the bigger pieces of wood.

Within a minute, they had a fire for dinner.

She sank to the ground and smiled. "Look at that."

Grandma Cecilia grinned. "You would make a good nomad. Ever think about road tripping around the States?"

Elana gave her grandmother a look. "I would love to travel, but I like my creature comforts, like my bed."

The older woman shrugged. "You'll be surprised at how well you will sleep out under the stars."

Elana cocked her head. "Grandma, have you slept under the stars?"

Her grandmother gave her a look. "Of course I have. When I was young. Now, let's get busy setting up camp. We'll have to go to bed soon since we are getting up early."

Elana was too tired to argue. She knew she was the one who was going to sleep out under the stars tonight. She couldn't very well let her grandmother sleep on the ground while she slept in the van.

"Do we have something to stick these hotdogs on?" Elana opened the back of the van and poked around under the seat for some skewers.

"We'll have to use sticks."

Elana cringed. "I don't think it's sanitary."

Grandma Cecilia picked up a couple of sticks off the ground. "We'll scorch them first and then stick our hotdogs on." She held the sticks over the fire. Before they burned, she pulled them back.

Elana held out her hand. "Here, let me do it."

Grandma Cecilia lifted her chin. "I can do it, Elana."

Elana took a deep breath. "I know you can. But as long as you are dragging me along on this road trip, don't you think I should take the opportunity to learn how to camp?"

A slow smile crept across the old woman's face. "You're right. Here you go." She handed over the two sticks. Elana wasted no time and stuck a hot dog on each one before she held it over the fire.

"Be sure to turn them. You want them to cook evenly," her grandmother called out from her position at the picnic table.

Grandma Cecilia pulled out two paper plates from a plastic bag that held the buns and chips. She already had two waters she'd retrieved from the cooler. "I don't think Anna put any mustard or ketchup in here. We'll have to eat the hot dogs plain. Let's make a stop tomorrow and get some more groceries."

Elana cut her eyes at her grandmother. "Or we could stop at a restaurant and eat a proper meal."

Grandma Cecilia brushed her off. "This is a proper meal, dear. Be grateful for what you have. Lots of people have less."

Elana felt a twinge of guilt deep down inside. She knew she came from a privileged background, and she tried to be mindful of that fact. "You're right, Grandma."

Once the hotdogs were cooked, she removed them from the fire and offered one to her grandmother, who captured a hotdog in her bun as Elana pulled the stick away. Elana stuck her hotdog in a bun and tossed the two sticks in the fire.

She sat down and wiped the sweat from her brow. "It's too hot for a fire in September."

Grandma Cecilia laughed. "You won't be saying that when we get farther into the mountains." She took a bite of her hot dog and closed her eyes in delight.

Elana took a bite of her hot dog. She was surprised by how good it tasted.

They ate dinner in silence, and when they were done, Elana gathered the items for her tent.

"Do you need help setting the tent up, Elana?" Her grandmother tossed their paper plates into the trash and began putting the food away.

"There are directions, and it looks relatively easy. I shouldn't have a problem." Elana lined up the tent supplies and the sleeping bag on the ground.

"I'm going to grab a shower while you do that. I won't be long." Grandmother Cecilia took a towel and her toothbrush along with a small bag of clothes.

Elana watched to make sure she got to the public showers okay before she started setting up her tent. She was a sweaty mess when her grandmother returned.

"You got it up." Her grandmother blinked.

Elana wiped her dusty hands on her jeans. "You sound surprised."

Grandma Cecilia chuckled. "I am. Now, you go get a shower and when you get back, we'll make sure the fire is out before we go to bed."

Elana looked at her grandmother. "Are you sure you can sleep in the van? I mean, the bench seat doesn't look very comfortable."

Her grandmother gave her a wink. "I'll be fine. Now go get cleaned up."

Elana didn't argue. She grabbed her stuff and headed to the shower. Kids were still splashing around in the pool while their parents sipped on drinks from red plastic cups. Elana wished she had a red cup filled with something that would help her sleep tonight.

Finding the showers empty, she locked the door before turning on the water. Quickly peeling off her clothes, she made sure the water was hot before stepping into the shower.

She stayed under the stream, letting the water wash away the day's sweat and dust.

She had only been on the road one day, and she was already tired. While they drove, her grandmother had chatted about anything and everything. But when Elana had broached the subject of her secret boyfriend, her grandmother quickly changed the subject.

Maybe her father was right. Maybe Grandma Cecilia

really was losing her ability to make sound decisions. The very idea made her heart squeeze in pain.

When her fingers turned wrinkly, she turned off the faucet and grabbed her towel. She dried off, brushed her teeth, and changed into some running shorts and a T-shirt to sleep in. Then she headed back to the campsite.

Her grandmother was already pouring a bucket of water over the simmering coals. A plume of smoke rose in the air, and the coals hissed.

When she saw Elana, she smiled. "Ready for bed?"

Elana stifled a yawn. "Absolutely."

Grandma Cecilia looked relieved. "Good. I already put your sleeping bag in the tent. I'll see you in the morning. Good night."

Elana hugged her grandmother. "Good night."

Once her grandmother shut the van door, Elana stepped into the tent and lay on top of the sleeping bag since it was too hot to get inside.

It wasn't long before she drifted off to sleep.

CHAPTER 6

*E*lana's eyes popped open. Though it was still dark outside, she heard the whisper of voices.

Sitting up in her tent, she unzipped the door and peeked out.

The voices belonged to a couple who were up early walking their German Shepherd. The play of the flashlight finally disappeared as they passed the campsite. Elana pulled her phone out of her sleeping bag. It wasn't even six yet, but she knew she would not get back to sleep.

Instead, she slipped on her shoes and climbed out of the tent.

The temperature was bearable this early in the morning, and the birds were beginning to chirp. She arched her arms over her head for a full stretch. The aroma of coffee had her mouth watering.

She couldn't remember if the office had a coffee station set up. Running her fingers through her brown hair, she walked over to find out for herself.

A few campers were already up and sitting at their picnic

tables. An older couple had set up their Blackstone grill and were heating it up to start breakfast.

Opening the door to the office, she stepped inside.

A different woman greeted her this time. She was in her late fifties and had flaming red hair.

"Good morning." Elana sighed heavily. "I was wondering if you had some coffee."

The woman brightened. "Just made a fresh pot. It's over there by the package of cinnamon rolls."

Elana padded over to the coffeepot and grabbed a Styrofoam cup. She poured her cream in before filling it with hot coffee. As she stirred, she looked out the window, watching the sky lighten.

"Where are you headed to? Anywhere special? Or is this your destination?" The woman asked as she straightened the stack of newspapers.

Elana looked over at her. "Montana."

The woman's eyes grew wide. "That's a long way from here. Are you camping the entire way?"

Elana shrugged. "It depends on my grandmother. The trip is her idea. I'm just the driver."

The woman laughed. "Sounds like your grandmother has spunk. Mine does too. She still cuts her own grass and drives herself."

Elana sipped her coffee. "That's impressive. I hope I have as much energy when I get that old. What's her secret?"

The woman's eyes sparkled. "She says traveling has kept her young. That's her secret. She goes on three trips a year with her girlfriends. I wish I had all that free time. I would travel too. The farthest I've ever been is Florida. Do you have family in Montana? Is that the reason for your trip?"

Elana took another sip. "No family. My grandmother has a... friend that lives out there." She didn't want to tell a stranger that her grandmother was being catfished.

"How sweet of you to take the time to drive your grandmother. You're a very good granddaughter." The woman smiled and then turned her attention to the young man who had just entered.

Elana topped off her coffee and fixed a cup for her grandmother. Surely she would be up by now.

After putting lids on the cups of coffee, she walked outside.

The sun was coming up, and she knew the heat would be unbearable within two hours.

When she got back to the van, Grandma Cecilia was sitting at the picnic table putting on her shoes.

"I brought you a cup of coffee." Elana placed it in front of her on the table. She glanced down at her shoes. "Grandma Cecilia, you have two different socks on."

This brought a smile to her grandmother's face. "I guess I do." She turned and grabbed the coffee. "Thank you, dear. Just what I wanted." She took a sip and then sighed contentedly. "And you made it just how I like it. Two sugars and cream."

Elana sat down across from her. "How did you sleep?"

Her grandmother took another sip of coffee and stretched her neck from side to side. "The bench seat certainly doesn't have much cushion. I'm hoping my friend in Mississippi will rectify it tonight."

Elana cradled the cup in her hands. "Do I know this friend?"

Grandma Cecilia barked out a laugh. "I don't think so, dear. Not unless you've been supporting a dog rescue."

Elana frown. "A dog rescue? What are we going to do at a dog rescue? Donate funds?"

Grandma nodded slowly. "Among other things. You see, Ethan, the guy who runs the rescue, is a military veteran.

When he got out of the military, he got a van and fixed it up. He's been all over the States."

Elana frowned. "I still don't know why we are stopping to see him. And you haven't told me how you know him."

Her grandmother took another sip. "I found him online."

Elana glanced away and muttered under her breath, "You meet many people online." She cleared her throat. "And you two are friends now?"

The older woman pulled a face. "It's not like that. He had a YouTube channel where he showed how to make improvements to vans to make them livable. He has a huge following online. He does it not to make money but to help people. People can stay overnight at the dog rescue in exchange for a donation to the charity. I want to see him so he can show us how to make the VW more comfortable for camping."

Elana wanted more information from her grandmother, but her phone buzzed.

She pulled it out of her back pocket and looked at it.

"Who is it? Your father?" Grandma Cecilia arched a brow.

"How did you know?" Elana arched a brow.

The old woman snorted. "He's checking up on me. Don't think I don't know what he is up to." She stood and grabbed her cup. "I'm going to the bathroom, and then I'm going to brush my teeth. We can grab breakfast when we fill up with gas. We need to be on the road and beat traffic. I'll be back."

Elana watched her grandmother walk to the bathrooms and picked up her phone.

Has Grandma changed her mind yet? Making any headway with her?

She grimaced at her Father's text.

She sent a quick text back. *We are headed to Mississippi today. She's still determined to go to see her friend. Talk later.*

Her father must have been satisfied with her answer because he didn't text back.

She had to admit it hurt her feelings a little that he hadn't asked about her and how she was doing.

Sometimes Elana couldn't help but feel she was born into the wrong family.

CHAPTER 7

"Hurry. We need to get to Harland Creek before the sun goes down. I already sent a Facebook message to Ethan that we were spending the night, so he's expecting us." Her grandmother glared at her as Elana finished filling up the gas tank.

"I can't help the fact that we must make so many stops. Maybe you should cut back on all those sodas you drink so we won't have to make so many bathroom stops."

Her grandmother glared and shoved her sunglasses back over her eyes.

Elana bit her lip to keep from grinning. There was no way Grandma Cecilia was going to give up her orange sodas.

She finally put the gas pump nozzle back and grabbed her printed receipt.

Sliding into the driver's seat, she shut the door. "How much farther does it say on Google maps?"

Her grandmother squinted. "Three more hours."

Elana started the engine, and they were back on the road.

She could almost swear that time seemed to have slowed down the last two hours they were on the road. Since they'd started the road trip, they had listened to three mediocre audiobooks.

Her grandmother wanted to start another, but Elana said she just wanted to listen to music.

They finally drove into the small town of Harland Creek just as the sun was setting. Once they were on Main Street, Elana pulled over and parked in front of a floral shop.

"What are you doing?" Grandma Cecilia glared.

"Grandma, the directions don't go any further. I'm going to stop and ask for directions before we get lost. Stay here. I'll be right back." Elana got out of the van and shut the door behind her. She walked up to the floral shop but stopped when she noticed the *Closed* sign. She continued walking down the sidewalk until she spotted a hair salon with two women milling about inside.

Elana glanced at the name of the salon and cringed. "Who would name their beauty salon S&M?"

One of the women, an older woman with short hair, noticed her staring at them through the door and came over and opened it.

"Can I help you, honey?" She smiled.

"I certainly hope so. I'm looking for directions to a dog rescue. I don't know the name or who owns it…"

The woman brightened. "You're talking about the dog rescue Ethan runs."

Elana nodded. "Yes, his name is Ethan. Can you tell me how to get there? It doesn't show up on my GPS."

The older woman laughed. "You won't find it on GPS because the place is barely a year old. Come inside and let me grab a piece of paper and write down directions. I'm Sylvia, by the way." She stepped aside so Elana could enter.

She smiled. "I'm Elana. I'm guessing you are the owner of S&M? Does the S stand for Sylvia?"

Sylvia beamed. "Yes, it does. And the M stands for

Maggie, my friend. She is in the back, closing everything down for the day." She pulled a notepad out of a drawer of the front desk. She scribbled some directions down and then explained them. Tearing off the piece of paper, she handed it to Elana.

"Thank you. I really appreciate it." Elana walked toward the door.

"Of course. Welcome to Harland Creek." Sylvia gave her a wave as she left.

When Elana got back to the van, her grandmother shoved her sunglasses back in her bag. "Did you find out where this place is?"

Elana took one last look at the written directions and then handed them to Grandma Cecilia. "Yes. It's out of town off a dirt road. So when we get close, help me look for it."

Within fifteen minutes, they arrived at a cabin located off the road. There were kennels near the house, and a very well-built man was shirtless and feeding the dogs.

"Hubba, hubba." Grandma Cecilia waggled her eyebrows.

Elana snorted. "Easy. Don't make me rat you out to your online boyfriend."

Grandma Cecilia shrugged. "No harm in looking. Come on." She opened her door and got out.

Elana braced herself and slid out of the van.

The man feeding the dogs wiped his hands off and grabbed his shirt off the fence. He pulled the T-shirt over his head and made his way over to them with a German shepherd at his side.

"Ethan Rodriguez?" Grandma cocked her head.

A smile played on his lips. "You must be Cecilia Taylor." He stuck out his hand.

Grandma Cecilia shoved his hand away and pulled him into a big hug. He laughed and wrapped his arms around her.

Elana felt her eyes grow wide.

"I'm so glad to finally meet you, Ethan." She turned to Elana. "This is my beautiful granddaughter, Elana."

Elana stepped forward and held out her hand. "Hi, Ethan. Nice to meet you."

They shook hands, and the door to the cabin opened. Out stepped a beautiful blonde woman who looked like she could have stepped off the cover of a high-fashion magazine.

Ethan turned and smiled up at her. "Baby, we have company."

The woman gracefully walked down the steps to the house. She gave them both a suspicious look.

"Cecilia and Elana, this is Felicia Dantry," Ethan announced.

Felicia gave them a cautious smile. "Hi, nice to meet you both."

Ethan barked out a laugh. "They are spending the night." His eyes darted over to the VW van. "That is a spectacular van."

Felicia followed his gaze. "It looks like the Scooby Doo van."

Elana bristled under the comment, but her grandmother barked out a laugh.

"Mind if I take a tour?" Ethan asked.

"Of course not. I was hoping you could give us some ideas of what to do to the inside to make it more comfortable to sleep in. I slept on the bench seat last night while Elana slept in a tent."

Ethan's eyes sparkled. "The possibilities are endless. Come on, let's check it out."

Grandma Cecilia followed Ethan out to the van while Elana hung back at the house.

"You slept in a tent?" Felicia arched her brow. "How was it?"

Elana ran her hands through her hair. "I kept waking up."

Felicia cringed. "I hate staying in a campground. Too many people. Now, boondocking is another thing. I like that better."

Elana frowned. "Boondocking? What is that?"

Felicia grinned. "When you camp out in the middle of nowhere. No electricity. No running water."

Elana shuddered. "That doesn't sound like fun."

Felicia barked out a laugh. "That's what I thought when Ethan asked me to go with him. But once we got into the mountains, it was wonderful."

Elana studied the woman. She didn't strike her as the outdoorsy type.

"Where are you headed to?" Felicia patted her leg, and the German shepherd ambled over. He sat obediently at her feet and let her stroke his head.

"Montana. We started in South Carolina." She kept her gaze on the large dog.

"Wow. You guys have a long trip ahead of you. And it's just you and your grandmother. Ever feel unsafe?"

Elana blinked. "I haven't really had time to think about it. This trip was a spur-of-the-moment thing."

Felicia nodded. "Come with me. I'll introduce you to our dogs."

Elana walked beside her over to the kennels. "I've never been to a dog rescue. How did Ethan start it?"

Felicia shook her head. "Ethan didn't start it. The town's veterinarian, Zander Howell, started it. He raised money to buy this house and the land with it for senior dogs and unwanted dogs to live out their days."

Elana's heart tugged. "Wow, that's very generous. And sad at the same time."

Felicia looked at her under her lashes as she unlocked the kennel door. "You're thinking it's sad that no one wants a senior dog or a dog with disabilities?"

Elana nodded and followed her inside the large kennel. It was self-contained, with separate rooms for each dog. Each room had its own bed and bowl of water, along with some toys.

She walked down the middle and looked at the dogs, who started barking with excitement when they saw they had company now.

"Do they stay inside all the time?" Elana asked.

"Oh, no. We just put them in here at night. It's a new building with heat and air, which makes it good in the summer and winter. Not all the dogs stay out in the kennel. Sometimes, if we have a dog that hasn't acclimated, we will keep them in the house with us and Ethan's dog."

Elana bent down and rubbed an older chocolate lab between the ears. "What happens if they don't acclimate?"

Felicia shrugged. "I don't know. Right now, we have a border collie/Siberian mix inside. His name is Jack. His owner went into the nursing home, and we took him in. We have been loving on him, but he seems depressed."

Elana stood. "That's heartbreaking. Did the owner not have any family that would have taken Jack?"

Felicia snorted. "He had two sons, but they didn't want a mixed dog. They only wanted a purebred."

It broke Elana's heart.

"Hey, you two. Are you up for a campfire?" Ethan called out as he and Grandma Cecilia poked their heads in the kennel. "I think the dogs want us to stop disturbing them so they can get some sleep."

Felicia laughed. "You're right. I was just trying to introduce Elana to our dogs."

Elana and Felicia walked out of the kennel and toward the house. Elana turned to Felicia. "So do the dogs ever get adopted out from here?"

Felicia grimaced slightly. "I'm afraid we are the last place the dogs go. Ethan is great with the dogs, and we have a pond behind the house, so he takes them for walks and lets them go swimming in the summer. He gives them the best life a dog can have."

Elana nodded. "You know, you said they are senior dogs. But they all seem like they have a lot of life left in them."

Felicia nodded. "They do. It just takes the right person to help them see that."

Ethan held the door opened while everyone walked inside.

A dog lying on a dog bed in the corner raised his head and looked at them before laying his head back down.

"That's Jack." Felicia walked over to a canister on the coffee table. She pulled out a dog treat and offered it to Jack. He sniffed at the treat and took it, but instead of eating it, he put his head back down.

"I wish I knew how to give Jack his puppy heart again."

Elana looked at him. "Puppy heart?"

Grandma Cecilia grinned. "Older dogs will usually get spunky once a puppy is brought into the house."

Ethan nodded. "That's right. Now let's grab these hotdogs and we'll cook them over the fire. You ladies like hotdogs?"

Grandma Cecilia grinned. "We love them."

After they ate, Elana pitched her tent outside while her grandmother slept in the van. And as she drifted off to sleep, she couldn't help but think about Jack and how she hoped he would find happiness again.

CHAPTER 8

ack stirred from his bed in the corner of the new house he'd found himself in.

He missed the old man who had raised him from a pup.

"Hey, Jack." The large man with the gentle voice came out of the kitchen with a cup of something hot in his hand. From the smell, Jack knew it was coffee.

The old man had drunk coffee every morning.

Jack lowered his head and looked at the large man.

"Let's go outside, Jack." The large man opened the front door and held it opened.

Jack slowly got to his feet and stretched his legs out in front. He walked over to the front door. The large man waited for Jack to walk out.

Jack looked up at the man. He had been nice to Jack, and even let him sleep inside instead of outside in the kennel with the other dogs.

But Jack was homesick. He wasn't sure he would ever get over losing the old man.

Jack let out a yawn and walked out onto the porch and down the steps.

Jack watched as the large man walked over to the kennels. The other dogs were barking and excited to see him. The noise was too much for Jack. He trotted off in the opposite direction.

Jack stopped suddenly. The air smelled different. He looked around and found the reason why.

There was a vehicle parked in the driveway, and it smelled old.

Jack trotted over and hiked his leg on the tire. Comforted by his action, he walked around the vehicle.

He stopped when he spotted a tent. The old man had a tent.

Jack stepped closer and sniffed the structure. He smelled someone inside the tent.

He poked his head in the small opening and cocked his head.

A woman with brown hair was sleeping. She moaned in her sleep and turned over on her back.

He nudged his way farther into the tent, placing a paw on her sleeping bag.

In her sleep, the woman seemed sad.

Maybe she had lost someone too.

She also smelled like a familiar scent, a scent he could not place. He stepped closer until his nose was touching hers and inhaled.

The woman opened her eyes. She opened her mouth, but nothing came out.

Jack licked her from her chin to her forehead. She smelled like Cheetos. They were the old man's favorite snack.

He cocked his head and gave the woman one last glance before walking out of the tent.

He slowly made his way back to the house, feeling a little less sad.

CHAPTER 9

*E*lana wiped her face with the back of her arm. She scurried out of the tent and watched the dog walk slowly back to the house after licking her full in the face.

It wasn't like she feared dogs, but it had been a shock to wake up to a dog standing over her.

She stepped on a rock and winced in pain. She ducked back into the tent to retrieve her shoes.

"Sleep good?" Grandma Cecilia popped her head out of the VW van.

"You're unusually chipper for this early in the morning," Elana groused.

Her grandmother stepped out of the van. "I had a great night's sleep. Ethan gave me a pad to put on the bench seat. He's going to help me make some improvements to the van before we go."

Elana froze. "Wait. I thought we were leaving today."

Grandma Cecilia inhaled deep. "We can stay a day or so. Depends on how much we get done to the van."

Elana shook her head. "The sooner we get to Montana, the sooner we can get home."

Grandma eyed her. "What's your hurry? What's waiting for you back at home?"

Elana shifted her weight. Her grandmother's words unsettled her.

"Come on, Elana." Her grandmother cocked her head. "Life is so short. And it's more than just work and being on a schedule. Believe me. I know." She turned and grabbed a small bag out of the van. "Felicia said it would be fine for us to shower inside. They don't normally allow it, but since I've been talking to her and Ethan online, they said we feel like they know us. Come on inside and get some coffee while I shower."

Elana crossed her arms over her chest and followed her grandmother inside.

Grandmother Cecilia greeted Ethan and Felicia, who were in the kitchen drinking coffee. Elana glanced over to the corner where Jack was curled on his dog bed. The dog spotted her and lifted his head for a second.

"Looks like you could use this." Felicia pressed a hot cup of coffee in her hand as Ethan escorted Grandmother Cecilia out of the room.

Elana looked at the beautiful woman. "Thank you." She took a sip and blinked.

"I added cream, but not sugar. If you need some, there's a container on the counter," Felicia stated.

Elana shook her head. "No. It's perfect." She looked back at Jack. "Does he always do that?"

Felicia followed her gaze. "Jack? Yes, he tends to lie around all day."

Elana shook her head. "No. Does he always wake people up in their tent?"

Felicia snorted. "Jack went into your tent?"

Elana nodded and sipped her coffee.

"Ethan, come here," Felicia called out.

Ethan appeared in the living room. Elana could hear the water in the bathroom running.

"Jack went into Elana's tent this morning." Felicia looked at him.

Ethan wrapped his arm around his girlfriend's waist and blinked. "He did?"

They were both staring at her.

Elana nodded. "He came into the tent and licked my face."

Ethan stared at her for a minute. "He did?"

She nodded and took a sip of coffee. "Yeah. He licked my face, stared at me for a few seconds, and then walked out of the tent."

Felicia snorted and looked up at Ethan.

"What?" Elana felt like there was something they were not telling her.

"Jack doesn't normally do that," Ethan stated. "Since we've gotten him, we've had over thirty overnight guests, and he won't go near any of them."

Elana shrugged. "Maybe he was curious."

Ethan shook his head. "I don't think that's it." He looked over at Jack, who raised his head. "I think he's drawn to you."

Elana frowned. "Me?"

Felicia studied her. "Do you have a pet at home?"

She shook her head. "No. I work too much to have a pet."

Felicia arched a perfect brow. "So, you're not opposed to a pet?"

Elana shifted her weight. "Well, I don't..."

Grandma Cecilia appeared in the doorway with fresh clothes on and a towel wrapped around her head. "What are you guys talking about? What did I miss?"

Felicia looked at her. "Jack is wanting to be friends with Elana. Seems like he came into her tent this morning and gave her kisses."

Elana cringed. "I wouldn't say a lick on the face is exactly a kiss."

Grandma Cecilia grinned. "She always wanted a dog."

Elana shook her head. "I don't think I said that."

Her grandmother sighed. "When you were a little girl, you asked for a dog for years." She rolled her eyes. "Your mother always refused because she didn't want a dog in the house."

Elana sighed. "That was a long time ago. I don't have time for a dog now. I work too much, and would hate for it to be alone that long."

Grandma Cecilia just stared at her for a second. "Things change, Elana."

Ethan broke the silence in the room. "Elana, why don't you go grab a shower. We'll eat and then start on some updates to the van that I think you'll both like."

Elana started to say they didn't have time to spend another day and that they needed to get back on the road.

But after looking at her grandmother, she knew there would be no changing the older woman's mind.

Instead, she plastered on a smile and headed toward the bathroom.

CHAPTER 10

*E*lana helped around the dog rescue while Ethan worked on the van and Felicia headed in to town. Her grandmother went with him to tell him exactly what she needed done to the old vehicle. Felicia came back around noon and took Elana and Cecilia to lunch while Ethan remained at home. They ate at the diner in the small town, and Elana was grateful for a home-cooked meal versus having to choke down another hotdog. Some older women started talking to them in the diner and offered to take them for a walking tour while Felicia went to show a client a house.

They were now back at the dog rescue and the sun was starting to set. Despite not making any progress on their journey, Elana and her grandmother had enjoyed their day.

Grandma Cecilia went to talk to Ethan while Elana helped Felicia with the dogs. As soon as she walked in the house, Jack stood up and walked over to her. He sat at her feet and stared.

"He never acts like that. I think he's choosing you." Felicia cocked her head.

"Choosing me for what?" Elana frowned.

"To be your dog." Felicia snorted.

The front door opened, and Grandma Cecilia burst into the room. "Elana, go look at the van. You won't believe it."

Grandma Cecilia stayed inside to talk to Felicia while Elana walked outside.

Elana couldn't believe her eyes when she saw the updates Ethan had done to the VW van.

"It's a real bed." She blinked as they stared into the van from the back door.

Ethan grinned. "I had to take out the bench seat to put this futon in. You can fold it up to make a couch, and the mattress is comfortable. I built out a platform for the mattress, and there's still storage underneath."

Elana's eyes grew wide. "Wow, that's incredible. Do you usually do this for people spending the night?"

He shook his head. "No, but your grandma told me when you were coming through and said she needed some help with renovations. She sent me money to buy the things needed ahead of time."

Elana watched as Ethan pulled out a drawer from the platform.

"I put your camping stuff in here. There should be enough room for you and your grandma to both sleep in this bed tonight if you want." Ethan stepped back so she could look.

"That's fantastic. And I'm sure Grandma Cecilia will love sleeping on an actual mattress."

Ethan nodded. "Come around to the side and let me show you what else I did."

She followed him and waited until he opened the side door. He stepped in first, and she watched.

"This is how you fold up the futon to make a couch." He lifted the mechanism to create a couch from the bed. He turned and looked at her. "And when you are ready for bed, just do this." He converted it back to the bed.

She smiled with relief. "My back thanks you, Ethan."

He barked out a laugh. "You're welcome. You ready for the other updates?"

She nodded and grinned.

He moved the futon to the couch position and then walked to the side of the van. "There is storage under the seat of the couch. I moved a better and bigger cooler here. So when you guys are boondocking, you'll be able to keep your food cold." He lifted the seat and showed her.

She looked at him. "And there's still room for other stuff."

He nodded. "You have your clothes in the small cabinets above the bed, but you could move your first aid kit down here."

Elana frowned. "We have a first aid kit?"

He grinned and pulled a kit out from beside the cooler. "You do now. Yet another item that your grandmother asked for." He put the kit back and let the bench down. "If you are thinking you want to make it solar in the future, you'd be able to do so. You could have a functioning refrigerator and some small lights. But for now, you can survive with what you have."

She arched her brow. "I don't think Grandma Cecilia will be taking any more trips in this van."

He cut his eyes at her. "What about you?"

She stepped inside and sat down on the sofa. "Me? I don't think I'm cut out for road tripping."

He studied her. "I don't know. You made it this far."

She looked down at the floor of the van and for the first time noticed the new item. "There's a rug."

He shrugged. "Not exactly new. Felicia found it at the thrift store in town. She picked it up today. She said she thought it might be just the thing to make your van seem more cozy."

Elana studied the green and blue rug. "It's beautiful. I'll have to thank her." She looked up at him. "Tell her she should be an interior designer. She has a great eye."

He grinned. "I will." He moved away from the side of the van where he was standing. "And now let me show you this."

Her mouth dropped. "That's a sink. How in the world can a van have a sink?"

He opened the cabinet underneath, revealing a large plastic water container. "It's self-contained. You just must be mindful of when you need to fill it up. Let me show you how it works." He turned the tiny handle by the faucet and demonstrated.

"That's great. Now to figure out how to heat my water for my coffee in the morning," she joked.

His eyes sparkled. "I put in a small water heater for future use. You still need to connect to electricity. But it's not for your coffee. It's for your outdoor shower."

She slowly stood up. "Shower? How is that possible?"

He slowly pulled out the extendable faucet. He stuck it through one of the jalousie windows. "Come outside."

She followed him around the van. He pulled out a plastic shower curtain from a bag on the ground.

"You attach the shower curtain to these hooks I put up. Once you step behind the curtain, you turn on the faucet and enjoy a shower."

She laughed. "That's incredible. I guess all I need is a fire to cook."

"Come with me." They walked back inside the van. He opened a cabinet under the sink. "That's what this is for." He pulled out a small gas tank and a portable stove. "This is a portable two-burner propane stove. You can use it outside, but once you guys get into the mountains and the temperatures drop, you'll want to make your coffee inside."

A smile stretched across her face. "As long as I have hot coffee, I think I can handle anything."

Ethan nodded in agreement. "I want to talk to you about something." He stepped out of the van. She followed, and he shut the van door.

"Okay." She shoved her hands in her jeans pocket.

"It's about Jack."

Elana looked at Ethan. "What about him?"

He glanced at the house. "Since you got here, he's been different. Better."

She followed his gaze. Jack was sitting on the top step of the porch watching them carefully. "I'm not sure it's me."

Ethan snorted. "Believe me. It's you."

Elana forced herself to look away from the dog. "I think you and Felicia are mistaken. Once we're gone, he'll forget about me."

Ethan cocked his head. "Are you sure about that?"

She opened her mouth to speak, but suddenly felt something against her leg. She looked down to see Jack resting his head against her leg.

Her heart tugged in her chest. "I can't stay." She rubbed the area behind his ears.

"I want you to consider something."

She looked at him and waited for him to speak.

"Would you be willing to take him with you to Montana?"

She started to shake her head. "I can't take him. What if he hates riding in the van?"

Ethan shrugged. "He loves riding."

She bit her lip. "What if he runs off or gets lost?"

Ethan shoved his hands in his jeans pocket. "Keep him on a leash."

She crossed her arms. "What if he gets sick?"

He cocked his head. "Just give me a call and I'll give you the closest vet. I'll even cover any costs he might incur."

She slowly shook her head. "Grandma Cecilia isn't going to go for this. It's her van, and I don't think she will allow me to take him."

Grandma Cecilia appeared beside her with a smile on her face. "I guess Ethan told you we are taking Jack on the trip with us."

Elana glared at her grandmother. "You already talked about this?"

She beamed. "Of course. I think it's a fabulous idea. We can drop him off on our way back from Montana. Besides, it's a good idea to have a dog for protection. You never know what kind of criminals are roaming the roads." She slapped Elana on the shoulder. "It's settled. Now come inside and let's eat. I made my famous lasagna."

Ethan and Grandma Cecilia walked toward the house, leaving Elana alone. She looked down at Jack. The dog stared up at her.

She knelt to Jack's level. Looking the dog in his eyes, she rubbed him between the ears. "I know we don't know each other. And I've never taken a dog on a road trip. Don't tear anything up, and don't run off. Deal?" She held out her hand.

Jack looked at her hand, took a step forward, and licked her from her chin to her forehead.

CHAPTER 11

$\mathcal{T}$he next morning, they were all gathered around the van. Felicia had brought Jack out of the house on a leash. She had his dog bed along with a bowl and some dog food.

Elana felt unsure about this whole situation as she took the leash from Felicia.

"What if he..." she started to say, but Ethan held up his hand.

"Just call if you have any questions or run into problems. Cecilia has my number. Call day or night," Ethan reassured her.

Grandma patted Jack's head. "He'll be fine. Once he gets on the road, he will be just fine."

Elana forced a smile. "Of course he will." She glanced down at the dog and then back up to the hosts. "Thanks again for having us. I'll be sure to tell everyone about this place and the good work you do."

Grandma nodded. "And I wrote a nice little check, which I left on the kitchen table."

Ethan shook his head. "Thank you, Cecilia. That's very generous of you."

Her grandmother shrugged. "Well, I can't take it with me. Might as well spread the wealth." She gave them both hugs before getting into the passenger side of the van.

Ethan squeezed Elana arm. "Don't look so worried. You'll be fine with Jack. You might even find he's a great help."

Elana nodded and said her goodbyes before loading Jack up in the back of the van. She walked around and got into the driver side and started the engine.

As they drove away, Jack looked out the back as if he were saying goodbye. He then curled up and lay down on the bed.

They made it two hours before Grandma Cecilia had needed a bathroom break. Elana wondered if Ethan should have installed a toilet instead of a working sink.

She managed to find a truck stop before pulling into a parking spot. Grandma Cecilia scurried out of the van leaving her alone with Jack. The old dog sat on his haunches and gave one sharp bark.

Elana looked back at him. "Need a bathroom break too?"

Jack cocked his head.

She nodded and grabbed the keys out of the ignition and walked around to open the side door. She grabbed his leash before he could jump out.

"The last thing I need is for you to run away. Ethan would be very upset if I let that happen."

Jack slowly got down from the van and she shut the door behind him. She walked over to a large grassy area near the interstate.

Jack lowered his ears as the noise rushed around him. Once he got on the grass, he seemed to freeze as his eyes darted about.

She knelt. "It's okay Jack. Ignore the cars. Just do your business and we can leave."

The dog looked at her and blinked. Maybe he understood her, maybe not. But he did his business right there.

She smiled and patted his head. "Good dog, Jack."

Quick as a flash he licked her from her chin to her forehead.

She cringed and swiped her elbow across her face. "There really is no need to do that you know."

Grandma Cecilia was out of the gas station and standing by the van. She gave Elana a wave to hurry her along.

Once everyone was back in the van, Elana started the engine.

"Everything go, okay?" Grandma Cecilia looked back at Jack.

"He did his business," Elana stated.

"So did I. We should be good for a while." Her grandmother grinned.

They made it to Arkansas and stopped in a town called Jonesboro, Arkansas. They pulled into the parking lot of a shopping center, and they got out to make a sandwich in the back of the van. Even Jack got a half a sandwich all to himself.

"Isn't this cozy?" Grandma Cecilia sat on the futon sofa next to Elana. "Tonight, we'll both be able to sleep on a proper bed."

Elana nodded. "I'll be grateful for that. But it might get hot."

Grandma shrugged. "It will be fine. I was hoping we would make it to Missouri by the end of the day." She pulled out her cell phone and showed it to Elana.

Elana took a bite of her sandwich and studied the map. "That shouldn't be a problem. Springfield Missouri is only four hours from here. We might even get further than that."

Grandma Cecilia beamed. "That would be great." She finished off her sandwich and dusted off her hands. "I'm going to find a bathroom in one of those stores before we hit the road." She grabbed her purse and climbed out of the van.

Jack jumped up on the sofa next to Elana.

She shook her head. "You're not supposed to be up here."

Jack cocked his head and then looked at her hand holding a Cheeto.

She arched her brow. "Smart dog." She held out a Cheeto, and he gently took it.

Elana finished her sandwich and was straightening the cover on the futon when Grandma Cecilia climbed into the passenger seat. "I'm ready when you are."

Elana nodded and grabbed Jack's leash. "I'm going to walk him before we leave."

Once they got on the road, Elana was determined to make camp on the other side of Springfield.

In the end, she did even better. She made it to Kansas City, Missouri.

It was dark when they pulled in to the small campsite. Instead of making a fire, Elana started up the two-burner stove top inside the van. She opened the side door of the van to let some air circulate and tied Jack's leash to the handle of the cabinet to keep him from running off.

She put the small skillet on the burner and began an omelet. She added tomatoes, green onions, and some mushrooms. When it was done, she took it to her grandmother, who was sitting at the picnic table.

"Thank you, dear." She smiled when she saw the meal. "I bet this is going to be good."

Elana grinned. "I hope so. I wasn't sure why you bought mushrooms at the grocery store, so I just put them in the omelet."

Her grandmother laughed. "I grabbed some for a salad. I figured we could have a quick lunch tomorrow." She glanced the van where Jack was sitting in the back seat looking out.

"Why don't you bring Jack out here with me. I can watch him while you finish cooking."

Elana frowned. "Are you sure?"

Her grandmother nodded. "Absolutely. Bring his dog bowl out. He can eat while I eat."

She walked back to the van, gathered Jack's bowl, and poured some dog food in. Grabbing his leash, she walked him over to her grandmother and handed it to her.

Elana walked back inside and began making her own omelet.

CHAPTER 12

*J*ack stretched his tired body. He noticed Elana didn't sleep very well. She kept tossing around in the small bed with her grandmother until she finally got up before the sun rose.

She quietly opened the side door of the van and stepped out.

Jack walked to the door and stared up at her. He didn't want her to be out in the dark by herself.

She cocked her head. "You couldn't sleep either?"

It didn't bother him that the reason he couldn't sleep was because she couldn't. She would probably say her sleeplessness was because of the heat. She'd opened the windows, and a slight breeze had stirred through the van during the night. Her sleeplessness wasn't due to it being hot. She was worried. He could smell it on her.

She clicked the leash on his collar and pressed her finger to her lips as she walked him out of the van to the picnic table. He tugged on the leash toward the grassy area, and she relented.

After he did his morning business, they walked back to their campsite.

"I need coffee, okay? So, stay here until I get the stuff out for it." She tied his leash to the wrought-iron picnic table and walked over to the van.

When she came back, she had a bag of coffee, a bottle of water, paper towels, a dishtowel, a campfire coffee pot, and something that looked like lint.

She knelt beside the fire pit. "We'll make coffee over the fire since I don't want to wake Grandma Cecilia."

Jack let out a yawn as he watched her build a small fire. Once the flames were high enough, she poured the bottle of water into the campfire coffeepot and set it over the fire on the grate. Elana sat at the picnic table they silently watched the fire.

He rested his head on her foot. She reached down and slowly scratched him between his ears.

Once the water began to boil, Elana stood and pulled the coffeepot off with the dish towel.

She placed a sheet of paper towel on top of her coffee mug and put some coffee grounds on the top. Slowly, she poured the hot water over the grounds.

When her coffee was ready, she sat back down beside Jack. They sat there in silence while she sipped her coffee.

"Jack, you're lucky you don't have family. It gets compli-cated sometimes. Not to mention that you are constantly wondering why you don't fit in."

He lifted his head and let out a whimper. He felt like he didn't fit in either. That's why they needed each other.

She rubbed the top of his head, and he leaned into her touch.

Elana pulled out her phone and sighed. "I was hoping to make it to Rawlins, Wyoming today, but that's almost a twelve-hour drive. I think we should just try to make it to Cheyenne. What do you think?"

He let out a small bark in agreement.

Elana chortled. "It's settled." She put her phone away while Jack lay at her feet.

They sat there together in silence with her drinking coffee and him drifting off to sleep as the sun began to come up.

CHAPTER 13

"We should cook steaks tonight." Elana glanced over at her grandmother. "I need a good solid meal. I'm tired of hotdogs and sandwiches."

Grandma Cecilia shrugged. "Let's make a stop at the grocery store and pick some up. We could even get one for Jack." She turned around and looked at Jack and gave the dog a smile. "You'd like that, wouldn't you, Jack?"

Jack let out a bark.

Elana laughed. "I'll pull into the grocery store coming up."

A few minutes later, she was pulling into a parking spot. "I'll run in. What else do we need?"

Grandma frowned as if she were thinking hard. "Get potatoes and ranch dressing for a salad."

Elana grabbed her purse. "What about dessert?"

Grandma nodded. "Yes. We need dessert. Get whatever you think would be good."

Elana nodded and slid out of the van. She hiked her purse on her shoulder and headed inside the small grocery store.

Grabbing a shopping cart, she put her purse inside. She went to the produce aisle and grabbed three large potatoes.

They had already had lettuce for salad, so she added a tomato and a cucumber to the cart. She quickly found the meat section and picked out some steaks.

She stopped by the dairy section and got some sour cream and cheese for the baked potatoes.

Next, she went over to the bakery and perused the cakes and donuts. She spotted an apple pie and settled on that. When she got in line to check out, she picked up a couple of magazines and put them in the cart as well.

After paying, she headed back to the van.

Grandma Cecilia was walking Jack on a grassy area. She noticed Elana and waved at her.

Elana opened the side door of the van and put the groceries away. By the time she was done, Jack had jumped up in the van beside her.

She grinned when she saw him wagging his tail in excitement.

"You are excited for dinner, aren't you?" She patted his head.

He let out a bark.

Grandma Cecilia laughed as she scrambled into the passenger seat. "How much longer until we get to our camp-site for the night?"

Elana shut the side van and walked around to the driver's seat. "A few more hours and we should be there."

It took longer to get there due to traffic. By the time they pulled into their camping spot, the sun was quickly going down, and the temps were considerably cooler.

"A fire is going to feel good tonight." Elana wrapped her arms around her as she went to the side of the van to let Jack out.

The dog jumped out before she could put his leash on. Surprising enough, he sat at her feet and didn't run off.

She grabbed the leash and quickly attached it. "Don't

scare me like that, Jack," she muttered as she walked him in the grassy area of their campsite.

"I don't think he would run off. Jack's a good boy," Grandma Cecilia called from inside the back of the van. She popped her head out and held up a hoodie. "Want to put this on?"

Elana shivered. "Yes. I guess you were right. I should have packed a proper coat." She and Jack walked back over to the van. Her grandmother held the leash while she tugged the hoodie on.

"That's better." Elana stuck her hands in the pocket. "I need to dig out that coat you brought for me."

Grandma Cecilia nodded. "I think Ethan stuck it under the platform of the bed. He rearranged things when he was making updates."

She nodded. "Jack has been walked. Do you want to sit outside while I start dinner?"

Grandma looked at her. "You're going to start a fire, right?"

Elana nodded. "I'll wrap the potatoes in foil and cook them in the fire while I cook the steaks on the burner inside."

Grandma Cecilia nodded. "Good idea."

Thankfully, the previous campers at the campsite had left a pile of wood behind. Elana began the job of stacking the wood in the fire ring. She added the lint and then lit the match. It didn't take long before there was a blazing fire.

Grandma Cecilia came out of the van with three potatoes wrapped in paper towels. "I prepped the potatoes."

Elana frowned. "Grandma Cecilia, you can't wrap the potatoes in paper towels. They'll burn. They need to be wrapped in aluminum foil."

Her grandmother frowned and looked at the potatoes. "Of course, how silly of me. I'll redo them." She went back inside and reappeared a few minutes later with the potatoes properly wrapped.

Elana smiled. "Thanks." She put them on under the fire and turned to her grandmother. "It should take some time for the potatoes to cook. I'll go and prep the steaks and salad."

Grandma Cecilia smiled and sat down at the picnic table. "Need help?"

Elana shook her head. "No. You relax out here with Jack."

Her grandmother smiled. "I think I'll catch up on some missed calls." She pulled her phone out and began texting.

Elana pulled the steaks from the cooler and found a plaster platter to place them in. She found some spices and some butter and let the steaks marinate while she turned her attention to making a salad.

Once the salad was made, she turned on the burner and began melting the butter in a small skillet over the burner. She realized how many supplies Ethan had added to the van when he made the upgrades.

The aroma must have drifted out from the van over to Jack. She heard him let out a couple of pitiful whimpers. She turned and looked out of the van.

His eyes were locked on her, and he cocked his head when they made eye contact.

She grinned. "Don't worry, Jack. We have an extra steak for you."

Grandma Cecilia patted the dog on his head. "He's just impatient. I can't blame him. Smells good, Elana."

Elana smiled at the compliment. "Thanks. By the time the steaks are done, the potatoes should be ready as well." She turned her attention back to the task of cooking.

Someone in the campsite turned on a radio, and the soft sounds of a country song drifted over her as she prepared their dinner.

She didn't normally listen to country music, but she didn't mind this song. She listened as the lyrics of finding one's place in the world resonated deep within her.

When the steaks were done, she plated them and carried them to the picnic table where her grandmother and Jack sat. Elana turned her attention to the potatoes on the fire. She slipped on a pair of oven mitts. After dragging the spuds out of the fire with a stick, she picked them up and carried them over to the picnic table, where she quickly unwrapped them.

Grandma Cecilia got up and headed inside. When she returned, she had some grated cheese, butter, and sour cream. "I'll finish the potatoes."

Elana nodded. "I'll grab the salads and some drinks."

Grandma Cecilia shook her head. "No, look under the bed. Ethan gave us a nice bottle of wine to enjoy. I feel like a nice cabernet with my steak."

Elana nodded. "That was nice of him. I'll grab it and be right back."

She headed inside and grabbed the two bowls of salad and topped them with the ranch dressing. She set them on the picnic table, then ducked back into the van. When she reappeared, she held two red plastic cups, a corkscrew, and a bottle of red wine.

Grandma Cecilia rubbed her hands together in excitement. "We are eating like kings tonight. Isn't that right, Jack?"

The dog sat on his haunches and gave a bark.

They both laughed as Elana struggled to uncork the bottle.

The quick popping sound as the cork was freed from the wine bottle had her grandmother applauding.

Elana poured the ruby liquid into each plastic cup.

A look of contentment washed over Grandma Cecilia's face. "This is the life, Elana. It's only going to get better as we head farther into the mountains." She took a sip of wine and began cutting her steak.

Jack let out a whimper, reminding her he hadn't been fed.

"Sorry, boy. I didn't mean to forget you." She pulled his plate close to her and cut up his steak before placing it on the ground beside him.

The dog ate with gusto while wagging his shaggy tail.

They enjoyed their dinner in silence, soaking in the ambience from the fire and the wonderful meal.

CHAPTER 14

*J*ack lifted his head when he heard the bark of
another dog. It was still dark, and he had to
squint through the small opening of the van
door to make out the tiny Chihuahua taking his owner on a
walk. He narrowed his eyes.

Elana and Grandma had slept on the bed in the van
together, while he slept on the floor. This time Elana didn't
toss and turn. It was probably due to the cooler temperatures. Grandma had suggested they keep the van door
cracked overnight to let the air circulate.

Before the old man went away, he used to take Jack on
road trips to the mountains. They would sleep in a tent,
catch fish, and enjoy being outside.

Jack wagged his tail at the memory.

Movement on the bed had Jack lifting his head.

Elana slowly crawled out of bed. She looked surprised to
see him watching her.

She pressed her finger to her lips in a gesture for him to
remain quiet.

Jack laid his head back down and watched as she slipped

on her coat and shoes and put a beanie on her head. She grabbed the items she would need to make fire. Snapping on his leash, she opened the door of the van and they both got out.

Elana turned and closed the door so as not to disturb Grandma Cecilia.

She grabbed some lint and built a small fire over the fire pit. Jack let out a whimper, alerting her that he needed to go for a walk.

"Sorry, Jack. I'm not ignoring you. Let's go for a walk." She set all her items down on the picnic table. and they scampered off to a nearby grassy area.

He trotted ahead of her, making it to the designated pee area.

He couldn't help but be distracted by all the different scents he encountered.

"Are you going to smell every area before you find the perfect spot?" she asked.

He stared at her and cocked his head. Didn't she know the importance of the perfect spot to pee?

Sometimes humans were so slow.

Finally finding a spot, he quickly did his business.

When they returned to their camping area, he settled in a spot near the fire pit.

Elana got busy pouring water into the campfire kettle. Once she started a fire, she sat the coffeepot over the small flames.

Settling into a seat on the picnic bench, she wrapped his leash around the leg of the table and sat back to wait for her coffee.

He liked this. The dancing of the flames and the crisp scent that carried on the cold morning air.

He let out a yawn, content with his current surroundings.

Elana reached down and scratched between his ears. He

decided to return the favor with a lick to the back of the hand.

She giggled and wiped her hand on her jeans.

That was good. Now she had his scent on her clothes and he liked that they were part of the same pack.

A few minutes later she was taking the kettle off the fire and pouring a cup of coffee.

Jack lifted his head when he saw a squirrel come out of a nearby tree.

"Don't even think about it," Elana warned.

Jack sighed heavily. She didn't realize how much he wanted to give chase to the squirrel. Instead of pursuing the rodent, he laid his head back down, content to just stare at the dwindling flames.

The light began to turn a shade of purple. It reminded him of how he and the old man would sit out on the porch of the old cabin waiting for the sun's light to touch the ground.

Jack thought life was full of unexpected twists and turns. After the old man left, he never expected to be back in the mountains. But fate had put Elana in his path, and here he was.

He looked up at the dark-haired woman and noticed how relaxed she appeared. He hadn't seen her like that before. It looked good on her.

Closing his eyes, he settled in for a quick nap before Grandma Cecilia woke.

CHAPTER 15

"*I* can't believe we have a flat." Elana bent to look at the blown-out tire on the van. They had barely made it out of Rawlins before the blowout occurred. Luckily, she'd pulled off as far on the shoulder as she could as soon as she realized the tire had blown. She stood and glanced at the passing cars, making sure they were moving to the far lane. The noise of the traffic along the highway was almost deafening.

"We have a spare." Grandma Cecilia stuck her hands in her coat pocket. "Let's change it and be on our way."

Elana shook her head. "We can't do that. I don't feel safe driving all the way to Montana on a spare. We're lucky it blew out a few miles from the city. I can put on the spare and then we will head back to town to get the tire replaced."

Grandma Cecilia pursed her lips and glared at her. "Are you sure you're not trying to come up with excuses to keep me from going to Montana?"

Elana looked over at her grandmother. "Why would you say that? I've come all this way with you. I made a promise to take you to Montana. Do you think I would lie?"

Grandma Cecilia seemed to study Elana.

For the first time in her life, Elana felt as if she didn't know her grandmother.

Elana clamped her mouth shut. The last thing she wanted was to get into an argument. Shoving her hurt feelings aside, she went to the back of the van and opened the door. She stood there for a minute, looking around for where the spare tire might be.

Elana gritted her teeth and searched for the tire. She felt a sense of satisfaction when she found it along with a jack and whatever the tool was called to get the lug nuts off the car.

Grandma Cecilia reached for the tire. "Here, let me help..."

But Elana gently pushed her away. "No. I've got it." She hefted the tire out and rolled it onto the ground.

Grandma Cecilia sighed heavily and parked her hands on her hips. "Have you ever changed a tire?"

Elana lifted her chin. "No, but how hard can it be?"

Her grandmother pulled out her cell phone. "I think we should call someone."

Elana blinked and pulled out her own phone. "I think I'll just google how to change a tire."

She quickly found a video on You Tube. Turning her phone around she showed it to her grandmother.

"If you really want to help, look up directions to the nearest tire place. Hopefully they can get us in quickly and we will be on our way."

Elana watched the video a couple of times before she felt confident enough to do it herself.

Grandma Cecilia sighed and then began searching for tire places on her phone.

Elana put the jack under the van, then attempted to raise the van enough to change the tire.

"Need some help?"

Elana jerked upright at the male voice. She had been so focused on the job she hadn't realized someone had stopped behind them.

She looked up at the old man in a cowboy hat dressed in dirty jeans, a plaid shirt, and muddy cowboy boots. Looking over his shoulder, she spotted the old pickup truck he was driving.

"We had a flat."

He grinned and shoved his hat back on his head. "I see that." He cocked his head. "Ever change a tire before?"

Lifting her chin, she crossed her arms over her chest. "I watched a video."

He chuckled. "I'm happy to help."

Elana was sure he was being nice, but she didn't want to appear helpless. "I think I can manage."

He took his hat off and scratched his head. "How about some constructive criticism?"

She narrowed her eyes. "Criticism?"

He barked out a laugh. "How did I know that was the only word you would pick up on? It's okay to ask for help, young lady."

Elana glanced over at Grandma Cecilia, who was watching them both carefully.

Elana cleared her throat. "Did you find a tire place?"

Grandma Cecilia shrugged. "There are three that I found."

The cowboy shook his head. "The only place I would use is Gadley's."

Her grandma frowned. "That didn't come up when I googled it."

He snorted. "If you want someone to fix that tire, Gadley's is the best in town. All the locals use them."

Grandma Cecilia looked at him. "Are you from here?"

He grinned and nodded. "Sure am. Born and raised. I have a ranch not far from here. Why don't you let me put your spare on and then you can follow me to Gadley's to have your tire fixed?"

Grandma Cecilia brightened and turned to Elana.

Elana was not as enthusiastic as her grandmother. But they were in a tight spot, and she didn't have much of a choice. "On one condition."

The cowboy cocked his head, waiting for her next words.

"You show me how to change the tire and actually let me do it. It will give me hands-on learning in case this happens again."

A big grin stretched across his weathered face, and he stuck out his hand. "Very smart of you. My name is Dennis. Dennis McClintock."

Elana took his hand. "Elana Taylor. This is my grandmother Cecilia."

He greeted them both. "Pleasure to meet you ladies. Now let's say we get this tire fixed."

Elana nodded. "Great. Just show me what to do."

CHAPTER 16

*E*lana peered out the window of the tire place as she waited in line. She spotted Dennis McClintock talking to a friend. For a small business, Gadley's was busy.

"Can I help you?" A middle-aged man in a dingy white T-shirt placed his hands on the counter.

She gave him a relieved smile. "I certainly hope so. We had a flat on the interstate, and I'm riding on the spare. I need to get my tire replaced as quick as possible."

He rubbed his eye and glanced back at the computer. "We are backed up with scheduled clients. I can fit you in at four o'clock this afternoon."

She blinked. "Four o'clock? Why, that's almost six hours from now. I need to be in Montana today."

The old man chortled. "Miss, I'm sorry. But there are customers ahead of you, and I have two men out with the flu. The earliest I can do is four o'clock."

Dennis came up beside her and smiled at the man. "Hello, Earle. Can you fix her tire?"

Earle sighed heavily. "I can fit her in at four."

Dennis took his hat off and rubbed his head. "I see."

Elana slowly nodded her head. "Fine. Four o'clock. I need to call around and find a place to camp tonight since it looks like we won't be leaving Wyoming today."

Dennis cocked his head. "You and your grandma camp in the VW?"

Elana nodded and pulled out her phone. "Yes. She is making me take her on this road trip and insisted we camp instead of getting a hotel. I'm not sure how hard it's going to be to find a hotel that allows dogs." She nodded toward the dog.

Dennis looked at Jack. "That's a fine dog you have. I bet he has some herding abilities in him. Looks like a border collie."

Elana gave a ghost of a smile. "They told me part border collie, part husky." She smiled at Dennis. "Excuse me while I call the campground we stayed at last night. Hopefully we can secure a spot tonight."

Dennis winced. "I don't think you will have much luck. Campgrounds around here usually stay booked."

Elana shrugged. "Well, I must try. Otherwise, we will be sleeping at the truck stop tonight."

Dennis shook his head. "I don't think that's wise. Not for two women."

She dialed the campground number and stepped away to talk.

What Dennis had said was true. There was no spot at the campground for them tonight. She quickly googled all the campgrounds nearby and contacted them.

They were all booked.

"Dennis told me we're going to have to spend another night here." Grandma Cecilia walked up with Jack in tow.

She glanced at Jack and her grandma. "Yes. They can't fix the tire until four o'clock. And I have more bad news."

Grandma Cecilia frowned. "What?"

She studied her grandmother. "There are no campgrounds available tonight. Which means we will spend the night at the truck stop."

Grandma Cecilia cringed. "I don't think that's a good idea."

She snorted. "Unless we find a hotel that allows dogs, then that's our only option."

Dennis walked up to them. "It's not your only option. You are welcome to camp at the ranch."

Grandma Cecilia's eyes grew wide. "Are you inviting us to your ranch?"

Dennis nodded. "Yes ma'am. I have a cattle ranch, and you can camp next to the barn."

Elana shifted her weight. "That's awfully nice, but we can't impose."

Grandma Cecilia elbowed her hard in the stomach. "Of course we can. I can't think of anything better than camping out with the cows." Her eyes shone with excitement.

Dennis chuckled.

Elana shot her grandmother a look, but she ignored it.

"You both can join my cowboys for dinner outside, and I'm sure Jack will love seeing the horses." Dennis smiled. "I talked to Earle. Instead of waiting around here until four, you can leave your tire to be fixed, and I'll send one of my cowboys into town to retrieve it. We can get it back on tonight, and you can head out early if you want."

Grandma Cecilia clapped her hands in excitement. "It's settled. Dennis, I can't thank you enough for your hospitality."

He dipped his cowboy hat and grinned. "You can follow me back to the ranch." He walked over to VW, took the flat tire out, and carried it to Earle, who took it in the back.

Grandma Cecilia started out the door and stopped. "Elana, what are you waiting for? Let's go."

Elana forced a smile and glanced down at Jack. The dog cocked his head. Jack was as nervous as she was about this new sleeping arrangement for the night.

CHAPTER 17

*E*lana parked the VW near the large red barn and killed the engine. Grandma Cecilia scampered out of the van, and she quickly followed. She walked around to the side and opened the door for Jack.

Without waiting for his leash, Jack jumped out of the van and ran over to the barn fence where a horse was tied.

"Jack! Wait." Elana ran after him, hoping the dog didn't agitate the horse.

Jack turned and looked at her like she'd lost her mind. Then he sat and looked up at the horse.

The large animal let out a whinny. Jack barked once.

"Looks like they are having a conversation," Grandma Cecilia joked.

Elana gripped the leash in her hand. "I need to get this on him, but I don't want to spook the horse."

Grandma grabbed her arm as she took a step forward. "Give him a minute. Let's find out how he reacts."

Elana shook her head. "What if he runs off?"

Dennis walked over to them and stopped. "I think he'll be

fine. He's been cooped up in that van for so long, it's good for him to stretch his legs."

Elana worried her lip with her teeth. "I don't know..."

Grandma nodded. "Dennis is right. Jack needs a minute to himself. In the meantime, Dennis, do you mind giving us a tour of your ranch?"

Dennis grinned. "It would be a pleasure. We'll take my big truck." He pointed to his large Dodge Ram truck parked in front of the barn.

Elana stood rooted in her place as her grandmother and Dennis walked toward the truck. She cleared her throat. "Jack, we are going to take a ride with Dennis to see the ranch. I know you are tired of riding, but I would like it if you came with us. Leaving you alone makes me nervous that you might run off."

Jack cocked his head and lifted one ear as if he were listening intently.

Elana forced herself to leave the dog and slowly walk toward the others. When she glanced down, Jack as trotting by her side.

"You're such a smart boy, Jack!" She petted his head.

"I knew that dog was smart." Dennis grinned when they approached. "Now let's see how he likes riding in the back of the truck."

Elana cut her eyes at him. "Is it safe?"

Dennis let out a belly laugh. "Ma am. We live on a ranch. Nothing is safe out here." He let the tailgate down on the truck. Jack walked over and put his front paws up.

"I bet there was a time when he could jump in the back of a truck. But like all of us, our old bones don't always allow us to do what we want." Dennis bent and picked up Jack and carefully placed him in the back of the truck.

Jack's mouth split with a grin, and he wagged his tail.

Elana's heart warmed in her chest. "He looks pleased with himself."

Grandma Cecilia wrapped her arm around her. "He sure does. Now help me up in this truck and let's go view the lay of the land."

Elana waited until Dennis closed the tail gate before helping her grandmother into the passenger seat of the truck. Elana climbed in the back seat.

When Dennis pulled off, Elana turned around to see Jack letting the wind blow his furry ears.

CHAPTER 18

*J*ack lifted his head in the air and sniffed.

Mountain air was the best.

But he liked ocean air too.

He couldn't stop wagging his tail as the man drove Elana and Grandma Cecilia around the pasture, where there were tons of cows grazing.

He liked the horse he met at the fence. He could smell that he was a good horse and not mean like some he'd seen in his life.

He was glad they'd had a flat tire. If they hadn't gotten a flat, they never would have made it to the ranch.

He liked how things worked out in life. Sometimes events were like a standing line of dominos. Jack loved watching the old man's grandson play dominos when he came to visit. Once one tile fell, it triggered the others. Once every domino had fallen, one could look back at the journey and see how many twists and turns it had taken to get where they ended up.

Sometimes by chance, other times by choice.

A low-flying blackbird cawed in the air. Jack lifted his head and barked in answer to the fowl.

After driving a bit across the massive land, they stopped. Dennis yelled, and suddenly a herd of large cows came toward the truck with a half dozen cowboys on horses.

Elana came to the back of the truck where he was sitting. He looked at her, barked, and wagged his tail.

"You certainly are enjoying yourself." Elana laughed and rubbed his head.

He nuzzled her hand, enjoying the sound of her laugh. She didn't laugh that often. She should do it more. It was nice.

The cows drew closer, and Jack stood up.

The cows came right up to the back of the truck. A black one let out a moo, Jack barked in return.

"They are looking for food. In the wintertime, we put hay out," Dennis explained to Elana and Grandma Cecilia. He lifted a hand and waved the cowboys over. "I want y'all to meet our guests for the night. This is Elana Taylor and Cecilia Taylor. They're going to camp out in their VW by the barn tonight. They had a flat, and it won't get fixed until late. So one of you needs to run to town this afternoon and pick it up. We'll get it back on the van so they can continue their road trip."

Jack felt Elana stiffen beside him. Jack sniffed the air but didn't sense danger. He wished Elana wouldn't worry so much.

One tall cowboy in a red shirt tipped his hat. "Nice to meet you both. I'm Sweeney." He then rattled off the names of the other six cowboys with him.

A smile broke across Grandma Cecilia's face. "Howdy, boys."

Elana just smiled.

"That's a nice dog you have there. Border collie?"

Sweeney rode his horse up to the bed of the truck and held out his hand.

"Border collie mix," Elana offered.

Jack sniffed Sweeney's hand and gave his knuckles a lick.

The cowboy tasted like beef jerky, so he gave him a second lick.

Sweeney laughed and scratched him behind the ears.

The horse looked down in the bed of the truck. Jack lifted his nose.

"Easy, Jack," Elana warned.

"It's okay, ma'am," Sweeney assured her. "They are just introducing themselves."

The horse snorted and rubbed her head against Jack's ears.

"Look at that. How sweet," Grandma Cecilia cooed.

"Anything to report?" Dennis asked Sweeney.

"We saw some wolf prints near the river. We'll keep an eye out to make sure the cattle are safe." Sweeney wiped his brow with the back of his arm.

Dennis nodded slowly. "Might have to start moving the cattle closer to the ranch where we can watch them. Let's put some of the newer cowboys on night patrol. Sleeping out under the stars builds character." He looked at Jack. "Isn't that right, boy?"

Jack let out a gleeful howl.

Everyone laughed.

He stopped to watch everyone's reaction and then wagged his tail.

"We'll head back to the ranch. We are cooking barbeque tonight. Hope you ladies like barbeque?" Dennis looked at them.

Jack could feel his mouth water at the mention of the word. The old man always liked to share his BBQ sandwich with him. They would sit on the back porch listening to the sound of the wildlife and eating in silence.

He missed the old man.

"Honey, we are from South Carolina. We love our BBQ," Grandma Cecilia crowed.

Dennis had let the tailgate down on the truck, and Elana was resting against it. Jack lay down and put his head near her. She reached over and rubbed his head.

Jack sighed. He knew this was peace. And it was something he hadn't felt in a while.

CHAPTER 19

*E*lana stood under the spray of the hot shower in the bunkhouse. Dennis had offered the use of the amenities, and she'd reluctantly agreed. But when she discovered how much privacy she would have, she jumped at the chance.

As she let the hot water wash over her, she thought back to the text she'd gotten from her father earlier that day. He'd wanted to know if she had witnessed any mental decline in Grandma Cecilia.

She sent a quick text saying she had not and then turned off her phone.

He hadn't asked how she was doing during the road trip. Not that it should be a surprise. He never really showed her much fatherly love. Anna was the only one who asked every day about their safety and how things were going.

She reached over and turned off the water. Grabbing a towel, she quickly dried off and changed into a gray lounge set. Then she picked up the hairdryer she dried her hair.

After slipping on her sneakers, she gathered up her stuff and headed back to the van.

"Ready to eat?" Grandma Cecilia called out from a picnic table.

"Be right there." Elana put her items away in the van and grabbed a coat. The temps had dropped in the mountains. She was grateful that her grandmother had gotten her a coat for the trip.

She got out of the van and shut the door behind her. She walked over to examine the new tire.

"We put it on while you were showering. This tire will get you where you're going." Dennis said.

Elana gave the man a grateful smile. "Thanks. How much do I owe for the new tire?"

Dennis shook his head. "Your grandmother already paid for it."

She smiled. "I appreciate everything you've done."

Dennis shrugged. "I have a daughter your age. I would want someone to make sure she was okay if she were on a road trip."

Elana's heart dropped. "Your daughter is lucky to have a dad like you."

Dennis chuckled. "I'm sure your father would do the same."

She snorted. "The most he might do is get his secretary to call AAA. But he wouldn't have the first idea how to change a tire."

He nodded. "City slicker."

She grimaced. "I don't think I've ever heard that word used outside of a movie."

Dennis grinned and waved her over to the campfire, where everyone was gathered around. "Come eat before it gets cold."

Elana didn't argue. The thought of food made her empty stomach rumble.

She followed Dennis over to the large table laden with

food. Elana picked up a paper plate and made a BBQ sandwich and added some baked beans and coleslaw to her plate. She snagged a small bag of Cheetos. She eyed the pound cake but decided to come back to get a slice.

Grandma Cecilia smiled and patted a seat beside her near the fire. Jack was resting contentedly at her feet, staring into the dancing flames.

Elana smiled and eased into the chair next to her grandmother. "How is it?" She eyed her grandmother's half-eaten sandwich.

The woman leaned close and whispered, "Don't tell them, but this is the best BBQ sandwich I've ever had."

Elana grinned at her grandmother's words. "That's high praise coming from you." She picked up her sandwich and took a bite.

The flavors of the sandwich burst on her tongue. She closed her eyes and sighed. Her grandmother was right.

A cowboy next to her chuckled. "Save room for dessert. We have the best cook in the state of Wyoming."

Elana smiled up at him. "Can't wait."

Jack looked up at her and whined.

"Grandma, did you feed him yet?"

Grandma Cecilia nodded. "Yes, but he's been smelling the BBQ. I wasn't sure if I should give him some or not. I certainly don't want an accident in the van tomorrow."

Elana met Jack's sad eyes. Her heart tugged in her chest.

She pulled off a piece of the sandwich and held it out for the canine.

Jack gently took it from between her fingers and ate.

"Good boy, Jack." She smiled.

The dog looked up at her, expecting more.

"Mind if I fix him a small plate of just BBQ? I promise I won't add any sauce." The cook, named Big John, knelt beside Jack and rubbed his head. Jack leaned into his caress.

"Are you sure it's no trouble?" Elana looked up at the large man.

"No ma'am. He reminds me of Thunder, my dog that died last year. I still miss him." A sad look crossed his face.

Elana's heart tugged in her chest. "I'm sorry to hear that. He sounds like he was a very special dog."

Big John looked up and smiled. "He was." He looked down at Jack. "You take care of him."

Elana nodded. "I will." She watched the man walk back to the table, where he busied himself making sure there was enough food.

"I think it's the other way around," Grandma Cecilia stated before finishing off her sandwich.

"What do you mean?"

She dusted off her fingers and shrugged. "I think dogs tend to take care of their owners. Jack is no different. I can tell by the way he looks at you that he is making sure you're okay."

She snorted. "Why wouldn't I be okay?"

Grandma Cecilia turned and gave Elana her full attention. "Maybe because for the first time in your life, you are starting to wonder about the direction your life is headed. And maybe you don't much like the trajectory."

Elana shifted in her seat. "I don't know what you are talking about. I'm not thinking anything."

Grandma Cecilia snorted. "Well, you should. Your family has never appreciated you, Elana. Don't think I haven't seen it."

Elana jerked her head in her grandmother's direction. "Did Father say something?"

Grandma Cecilia stood and let out a laugh. "Your father would never have a genuine conversation with me if his life depended on it."

She shook her head. "Even as a child, he was always up to something." Her eyes narrowed. "Sneaky like his father."

Elana, intrigued at to her grandmother's words, stood. "You don't ever really talk about Grandfather."

Grandma Cecilia leveled her gaze at Elana. She locked her arm with her. "Come on. Let's go visit the horses. I'll tell you a story. About my past."

CHAPTER 20

*E*lana's ears tingled. Her grandmother had never talked to her about her past. When she was growing up, she would find old pictures and ask about the people in them, but Grandma Cecilia would always say she didn't remember who they were.

They stopped at the arena, where some cowboys were working their horses. "Say, Elana, that's a good-looking cowboy over there." She pointed a slender finger at the tall cowboy dressed all in black. He had his cowboy hat pulled low over his eyes. He twirled the rope over his head and lassoed a calf.

Impatient Elana looked back at her grandmother. "If you say so."

Her grandmother eyed her. "You know, if you don't slow down and enjoy the scenery, it's all going to pass you by."

She squinted. "What's going to pass me by?"

Grandma Cecilia gently touched the end of her nose. "Life." She turned and slowly made her way over to some folded chairs and eased into one of the seats.

Elana snorted. "You act like I'm not doing anything with

my life. I have a job, you know. A job that could fire me while I'm away on this trip with you."

Grandma Cecilia looked up at her. "Elana, are you happy with your job?"

Elana plopped down in the chair and sighed heavily. "What does happiness have to do with work?"

Her grandmother cocked her head. "It has everything to do with it. When you are in a miserable job, if affects your whole health." She looked out into the arena. "A bad job is like a toxic marriage."

Elana looked at her grandmother under her lashes. "Are you talking about your marriage? Do you think your marriage to Grandfather was toxic? Is that why you found someone online?"

Her grandmother looked at her and smiled. "Yes. That's exactly why I am talking to someone online. The only thing wrong with your statement is you said I found him." A slow smile grew on her lips. "It's quite the opposite, dear. He found me on Facebook."

Elana's heart dropped. "That's exactly what I was afraid of."

Grandma Cecilia barked out a laugh. "What's wrong with a man finding the woman he loves?"

Elana shoved her hands into her jacket pocket. "You don't even know this man. Maybe Father is right. This man is after your money."

Her grandmother turned and studied her. Elana expected to see hurt in her eyes, but instead she saw resolve.

Grandma Cecilia narrowed her eyes. "I never loved your grandfather. And he knew it."

Elana blinked, shocked at this revelation. "Then why in the world would you marry him?"

The older woman snorted. "It was expected of me. You see, my parents were poor. Dirt poor. And I had the one thing they could barter for wealth. My looks." She eyed Elana. "It may not look like it now, but I was quite the beauty in my day."

Elana smiled. "You've always been pretty, Grandma Cecilia."

That brought a smile out of the older woman. "In my prime, I was stunning." She looked back at the star-filled sky. "And boy, did I know it." She smirked.

Elana grinned. "Did you have a lot of admirers?"

Her grandmother lifted her chin. "Of course. But there was only man for me. Ronald Beckwith." Her eyes lit up as she spoke.

Elana had never seen her grandmother look like a giddy schoolgirl. "Tell me about him."

Grandma Cecilia sighed and leaned back in her chair. "He was tall and broad, much like those cowboys over there." She pointed to a large cowboy riding a horse in the arena. He spotted them staring at him. He grinned and tipped his hat.

Elana slapped her grandmother's hand. "Stop pointing."

The older woman giggled. "You need to stop being so scared of having a man look at you, Elana. You need to live a little."

Elana felt her face heat, and she turned away.

"I met Ronald when I was a senior in high school. He'd just moved there. His parents were killed in a car accident, and he was sent to live with his grandparents." She smiled as she recalled the memory. "The first day he walked into the school, we locked eyes. It was electric. I knew then there would never be another man for me." A sadness etched into her face. "But then my parents found out about us and demanded we break it off. They said Ronald was poor and would never amount to anything. But I held my ground. I defied them. Until one Sunday afternoon…"

Elana studied her. "What happened?"

Her grandmother swallowed hard, and she studied the ground. "My father came in the house with an envelope. He handed it to me and said he was right about Ronald. He said that Ronald was untrustworthy, and he was cheating on me. I pulled out the picture to see Ronald hugging another woman. The picture had been taken at a restaurant in Charleston. I was devastated."

Grandma Cecilia looked at her. "When he came over for our date that night, I broke it off with him. He wanted to know why, but I told him I had my pride. As he was leaving, my father told him that no daughter of his would marry someone who would never amount to anything."

Elana gasped. "That's pretty cruel."

Grandma Cecilia nodded. "I never saw him again after that. The rumor was his grandparents let him move to his uncle's in Montana."

Elana cocked her head. "Is that when you met Grandfather?"

Her grandmother rolled her eyes. "John Taylor was a couple of years older than me. When he found out I was single, he came to the house to ask my father if he could court me." A slight smirked played on her lips. "I believe you young people call that dating."

Elana snorted. "I've heard the term."

Grandma Cecilia drew in a deep breath and blew it out. "After that, things moved quickly. John asked for my hand in marriage, and my father gave his permission."

Elana bristled. "What about you? What did you want?"

Her grandmother turned her tired eyes on her. "I didn't want to get married, not after Ronald left. But my parents were poor and desperate for money. They saw dollar signs when John Taylor entered the picture. I didn't put up much of a fight. I was too heartbroken over Ronald. I barely remember the wedding."

Elana shifted in her seat. "Were you okay? I mean, he didn't hurt you, did he?"

Her grandmother shook her head. "John didn't hurt me. He was too caught up in trying to invest his money in the latest idea. My parents passed away thinking we were rich. But the truth was John had wasted his inheritance and gotten us deep in debt. When he passed away, it was kind of a blessing." She cut her eyes at Elana. "I guess you think that's a horrible thing to say."

Elana shrugged. "I have no right to comment. I wasn't in your shoes."

Her grandmother relaxed. "Anyway, after he passed, I put all my focus into making the business successful. And I did just that."

Elana studied her grandmother. "So now you're starting to think about the past, and you're getting sentimental about the romance you missed out on. And you find someone on the internet." She nodded her head. "Grandma Cecilia, that all makes sense. It's hard to lose the one person you thought you would end up marrying. But finding someone on the internet is dangerous. I mean, you don't even know this guy."

Her grandmother stood and looked at her. "Elana, I'm not going to waste the rest of my life not following my heart. I'm dead set on this, and there is no changing my mind."

CHAPTER 21

*E*lana felt like she'd been hit by a two-by-four. She leaned closer to her grandmother. "What about your home? Your business? Your family? It's all in South Carolina, and this guy is in Montana. How is this ever going to work?"

Grandma Cecilia shrugged. "It always works out in the end, Elana."

Elana shook her head. She couldn't believe what her grandmother was saying. Her hardworking, honorable, salt-of-the-earth grandmother was now tossing everything to the wind for some stranger she didn't know.

Elana couldn't listen to any more of this foolishness. She stood up and stormed away.

The cold night air sent a shiver through her body, and she snuggled down deep in her coat.

She stopped at a large oak tree. Something brushed against her jean-clad leg, and she looked down.

Jack had followed her and nuzzled his face against her to comfort her.

She smiled and knelt to give the dog some pets.

"Hey, Jack."

The dog nuzzled her face with his snout. She pulled him into a hug.

She eased to the ground, and Jack, as if sensing she needed comfort, crawled into her lap and rested his head on her shoulder.

They sat there like that for what seemed like an eternity. And that was okay with Elana.

* * *

JACK SENSED the emotions rolling through Elana, like waves on the ocean. Jack liked the ocean. The old man had taken him there once on one of their travels.

That was when he was young. Now that he was old, he wasn't so sure the dampness of the beach wouldn't soak into his tired bones.

The ocean was quite different from the mountains. The mountains always made him feel alive with the crisp air and sharp scents.

He wished he'd lived in the mountains forever.

He felt Elana began to relax, and her emotions shifted from anxious to calm.

He sighed and curled into a ball in her lap. Resting his head on her thigh, he closed his eyes and dreamed of many more adventures with Elana while he still had the time.

CHAPTER 22

$\mathcal{E}$lana woke up before Grandma Cecilia. The temperature had dropped during the night, but they had slept under the warmth of the quilts that her grandmother had had the foresight to pack. Sometime during the night, Jack had snuck into their bed and curled up at their feet, keeping them warm. It wasn't until Elana tried to turn over but was trapped under Jack that she decided to go ahead and get up. Sitting up in bed, she eased her feet out from under Jack.

The dog lifted his head, blinked, and lay back down.

She grinned and shook her head. Placing her feet on the floor of the van, she shivered and grabbed a pair of wool socks off the floor. After getting dressed as quietly as possible, she slipped her coat on.

Elana set the coffee kettle on the small propane burner and turned it on. She grabbed her mug and creamer out of the cooler and waited patiently for the coffee to be ready.

Jack lifted his head and sniffed before lying back down on the bed.

Once the coffee was ready, she poured herself a cup and

mixed in some creamer. She crept to the van door and opened it. Stepping out into the cool morning air, she shivered.

She turned to shut the door and found Jack standing there.

"Come on, boy," she whispered. The dog bounded out of the van.

The campfire from the night before was long gone. She spotted some cowboys saddling up their horses in the arena. She decided to walk over and sit in one of the chairs she'd sat in with her grandmother last night.

She took a sip of her coffee and let the liquid warm her from inside. Jack sat in front of her watching the horses with curiosity.

Her grandmother surprised her last night. She'd always known her grandmother to be a driven businesswoman. But last night she talked like a woman in love.

A part of what her grandmother said resonated with her. She knew what it was like to try to live up to her family's expectations. Never had they asked what made her happy. She'd even gone into advertising to help with the business. But she soon learned her family preferred someone with more experience, so she settled for whatever clients came her way.

Since her birth, her family had instilled in her the idea that supporting the Taylor business was number one.

Jack arched an ear as a cowboy rode over.

Embarrassed that she had literally just rolled out of bed, Elana smoothed down her hair.

"You're up early." The cowboy grinned.

She swallowed. "I could say the same about you."

A slow grin crossed his lips. "I didn't get a chance to introduce myself yesterday. My name is Riley Hartness." He tipped his hat.

She grinned and stood. "I'm Elana Taylor. Nice to meet you."

He cocked his head. "You wouldn't be related to the Taylors who run that big outdoors operation in South Carolina? Taylor Outfitters?"

She ducked her head. "I'm afraid so. My grandmother started the company."

His eyes grew wide. "Wow, I didn't know. Do you work at the company?"

She shifted her weight. "Indirectly. I help support the family with different charities. I work at an advertising agency."

He grinned. "Oh yeah? Any clients that I've heard of?"

Elana shook her head. "Probably not."

"So, Elana, what do you do for fun when you're not working? Spend the night in a VW van?"

She felt her face heat at his teasing. "Actually, no. This is a first. And the first road trip I've ever taken. Is your horse friendly?" she asked, desperately wanting to change the subject.

"He is. You can pet him if you want."

She reached out and stroked his long face. The black horse nuzzled her fingers.

"Do you ride?"

Elana shrugged. "It's been a while. I haven't been on a horse since I was little. I didn't have much opportunity."

He cocked his head. "Too busy with work?"

She grinned. "Something like that."

The cowboys near the barn called out to round everyone up. Riley turned and nodded to his boss. "Well, Elana. It was nice meeting you. I hope you have a safe journey on to Montana. And whenever you get the chance to ride, don't pass it up." He grinned and rode back to the rest of the cowboys.

Elana watched as the cowboys rode out into the pasture and off into the sunrise.

She finished off her coffee and headed back to the van with Jack in tow.

Maybe Riley was right. Maybe she'd already passed on some of life's opportunities.

But if her grandmother was right, there was still time.

CHAPTER 23

They hit the road after the cowboys shared their breakfast with them. Elana was glad she didn't eat as much as her grandmother. If she did, she would be in a food coma. An hour into the road trip, Grandma Cecilia ended up crawling back into bed for a nap.

Elana looked in her rearview mirror at the image of her grandmother sleeping comfortably in the back. She glanced over at the passenger seat, where Jack was sitting watching with excitement.

The older dog had wasted no time in climbing into the empty seat, and Elana didn't bother stopping him.

Her phone buzzed just as she put on an audiobook. She reached for the phone and looked at the message.

Call me.

She sighed heavily at her father's message. She had been letting his calls go to voicemail. When he sent a text, she would only reply with short yes and no answers.

Her phone buzzed again.

Now, Elana.

Her gut twisted as she dialed his number. He answered on the first ring.

"Hi, Father."

He growled slightly before he spoke. "Why haven't you been answering my phone calls?"

She plastered a fake smile on her face and answered as cheerfully as possible. "Because we are in the mountains and the service is spotty. We spent last night in Wyoming and should be in Montana this afternoon." She cast a worried glance at Jack.

"Where's your grandmother?"

She glanced in the rearview mirror to make sure Grandma Cecilia was still sleeping. "She's taking a nap."

Her father grunted. "Is she sick?"

Elana shook her head. "No. She ate too many pancakes this morning and is in a sugar coma. Other than that, she is as healthy as a horse." She glanced at the time.

"I can't believe she would just take off on a whim to meet some stranger she has built up in her head. Well, not to worry. By the time you both get back, I will have all the paperwork ready for her to go into a nursing home."

Elana frowned. "I thought you said assisted living?"

Her father cleared his throat. "Yes, of course. That's what I meant. Keep me updated on when you start heading back here."

Before she could answer, he had ended the call.

She glared at the phone and tossed it onto the seat beside Jack.

The dog looked down at the phone and pawed at it until it fell on the floor.

She gave the dog a scratch behind the ear. "Good think-ing, Jack. We don't need any more distractions, do we, boy?"

Jack licked the back of her hand and then looked straight ahead out the window.

CHAPTER 24

*J*ack was grateful for the stop at the turnoff. They'd driven for hours, and when they'd crossed over into Montana, Grandma Cecilia decided she wanted to fix a sandwich. Elana found the next turnoff and took him for a long walk in the grassy area.

Jack's ears perked up when he heard an unusual sound. He jerked his head in the direction it was coming from.

He spotted two rodent-like animals sitting in a hole and "chattering" to each other.

Jack let out a bark. The two ground squirrels' chatter intensified.

"Oh my gosh. Those are prairie dogs." Elana gasped. "I've never seen a prairie dog."

Jack looked up at Elana. She must be seeing things.

Jack knew his own kind, and those two things were not *dogs*.

Elana turned and called back to the van. "Grandma Cecilia, come see."

Jack kept his eyes on the two fat squirrels and growled.

"What's going on?" Grandma wiped her hands on a dish towel she was holding.

Elana pointed. "Look, prairie dogs."

Jack barked in disagreement. Why would Elana think those two creatures were dogs? Maybe she needed glasses. The old man had to start wearing glasses when he got old.

"I'm going to get a picture." Grandma Cecilia pulled out her cell phone from the pocket of her jeans.

Suddenly, another large squirrel poked his head out of another hole.

They were being surrounded! He had to protect Elana and Grandma Cecilia!

Jack let out a string of barks and tugged at the leash.

"Jack, calm down."

How could she not see they were being surrounded? He had to take matters into his own hands. Tugging as hard as he could, he pulled the leash out of Elana's hand and raced toward the large ground squirrels.

Elana screamed behind him, but he was on a mission. He had to protect his family!

Letting out a string of barks, he raced toward the fat ground squirrels. He was almost at the hole they were sitting in when they suddenly disappeared.

Sticking his snout into the hole, he started digging.

"Jack, stop!" Elana screamed.

He could smell the animal and knew he was close to capturing it.

Then something bit him. He let out a yelp and backed out of the hole.

Elana knelt beside him. "Grandma, he's got a red mark on his nose. I think the prairie dog bit him."

Jack's heart was pounding in his chest at the excitement. The pain was subsiding, but Elana was holding him close, and Grandma Cecilia was calling someone on her phone.

"There's a vet twenty miles away. I'll text Ethan and have him send Jack's up-to-date paperwork to the vet, so they'll be ready for us when we get there."

Elana lifted Jack up in her arms and held him close.

"It's okay, Jack. We'll get you looked at." She looked at Grandma Cecilia. "You don't think prairie dogs have rabies, do you?"

Grandma Cecilia gave her a worried look. "I don't know, Elana. But the vet will help him."

Jack whimpered at the word "vet."

He might be only a dog, but he sure knew who the vet was. And it wasn't good.

CHAPTER 25

*E*lana lost only a few hours at the vet. The doctor said it was not a bite, only a scratch. Jack was up-to-date on his shots, and they left the vet with some antibiotic ointment and a wallet that was a hundred dollars lighter.

Now back on the road, Elana could feel her grandmother's gaze on her as they wound their way through the mountains to their destination. She had put on an audiobook, which usually kept Grandma Cecilia's attention, but today felt different.

She cleared her throat and turned down the volume. "So, are you excited?" She cut her eyes at the older woman.

Her grandmother blinked, and then a slow smile stretched across her face. "I am. It's been a lot of years since we've seen each other. We've both changed a lot, I'm sure."

Elana glanced at her. "You're still a beautiful woman, Grandma Cecilia. He'll be impressed when he sees you."

Her grandmother brightened. "Thank you, dear." She gave her a knowing look. "You know, you're quite a looker yourself. I'm surprised you've not found the love of your life."

Her shoulders slumped. "Please don't try to sell me that. I

am aware I'm not gorgeous like my sisters. They are the ones who won beauty pageants."

Her grandmother huffed. "You would have won as well if you'd entered."

She shifted in her seat. "Father told me not to bother. He said it would be a waste of time, and I didn't have a chance of winning anyway."

Grandma Cecilia turned in her seat and gaped at Elana. "Your father actually said that?"

Elana nodded. "Yes. I mean, he was right. I surely wouldn't have won, and probably wouldn't even have placed."

Her grandmother's face turned beet red. "The gall of that man. I can't believe I raised such an insensitive idiot."

Elana was shocked by the outrage from Grandma Cecilia on her behalf. She swallowed. "It's no big deal."

Her grandmother narrowed her eyes. "What about when you quit guitar lessons? Was that your idea?"

Elana didn't like the turn of the conversation.

"Elana, answer me truthfully."

She sighed heavily. "Mother made me quit. She said getting to my lessons interfered with her tennis lessons."

Grandma Cecilia tightened her hands into fists. "Elana, I wish you had told me."

She shrugged. "It wouldn't have mattered."

The older woman lifted her chin. "It would have made all the difference in the world. Did you know that Elizabeth and Brianna both came to me and told me they wanted to take gymnastics? Your mother wanted them in ballet, but after I had a talk with her, she consented. I may be old, Elana, but I still hold a lot of power in this family."

Elana's shoulders slumped a little. "I guess I just wanted so much to please my parents that I didn't argue with them."

Grandma Cecilia said, "You need to learn to stand up for

yourself more, honey. I know being the oldest you have a lot to live up to...."

Elana snorted. "Not exactly."

Her grandmother whipped her head around in her direction. "What do you mean?"

Elana shrugged. "I mean, I know that Mother and Father had Brianna and Elizabeth to make up for how I turned out."

Her grandmother's eyes bugged out of her head. "What in the world gave you that ridiculous idea?"

Elana glanced out the driver's side window and went quiet.

"Elana, answer me."

She took a deep breath and let the words tumble out. "I overheard my parents tell one of their friends they were thankful that Brianna and Elizabeth turned out well, since I didn't live up to their expectations. They were in the kitchen, and I had popped over to bring some paperwork that Father had asked me to bring over. I was too embarrassed to let them know I was there, so I ended up leaving the paperwork on the foyer table and sneaking out before they could see me."

Thick silence filled the interior of the vintage van.

"It's no big deal. I got over it," Elana stated.

"It is a big deal. I should have been more involved in what was going on. Instead, I was running the business. I say that family is everything, but I certainly haven't acted like it. For that I'm sorry, Elana." Her grandmother reached over and squeezed her leg.

The kind words made Elana look away. She wasn't used to so much affection.

"Let's turn the audiobook back on. I want to see what happens to the man that left his wife." Her grandmother gave a forced smile.

Elana nodded. As the audiobook played, Elana let her

mind wander. She couldn't help but wonder how different her life could have turned out with a just a few different decisions.

CHAPTER 26

"We are getting close," Elana announced when she spotted the state sign welcoming them.

Jack let out a bark, but her grandmother grew silent.

She looked over at her. "Everything okay? I thought you would be excited."

Her grandmother glanced down at her flannel shirt and jeans. "Elana, look at me. I can't see Ronald looking like a lumberjack. We need to find a store so I can pick up something nice." She picked up her phone and begin googling boutiques.

"Are you serious? Surely he doesn't expect you to be in an evening gown and heels."

Her grandmother pursed her lips and glared. Elana knew from the daggers her grandmother was shooting at her not to argue.

Giving up trying to reason with her, Elana stared straight ahead. "Give me the address."

An hour later, they were pulling off the interstate to a city. Following directions, she quickly found the upscale boutique. She parked and grabbed Jack's leash.

"I'm going to walk Jack across the street at that park while you shop."

Grandma Cecilia grabbed her purse. "I won't be long. Keep your phone with you in case I need help deciding on an outfit."

Elana nodded and climbed out of the van with Jack in tow. She waited until her grandmother disappeared into the boutique before continuing her way to the grassy area with the canine.

She watched as Jack walked around, taking his time to sniff different areas before settling on a place to do his business.

"That's a pretty dog you have." A man with dark hair and wearing a hoodie slowly approached her.

Elana glanced at Jack and then back at the man. "Thank you."

His dark eyes were trained on her. The wind changed direction, and she caught his unwashed scent. The hair on the back of her neck stood at attention, and something inside her told her to run away.

"Are you done, Jack?" she called out.

"What's your hurry? You must be new in town." A slow grin stretched across his tobacco-stained teeth, and he took a step closer.

She turned her back to leave when she felt his hand clamp down on her arm.

"That's rude. You can't leave. I'm not done with you."

Fear clawed its way up her throat and came out in a scream. He slammed his dirty hand across her mouth and wrapped his arm around her waist to keep her from drawing attention from people. In her attempt to get away, she dropped the leash.

Suddenly Jack let out a growl and raced toward them.

From the corner of her eye, she saw Jack launch himself at the stranger and bite him on the arm.

The man let out a yell and released her. He cradled his arm and stared down at the growling and barking dog in fear.

The stranger began backing away while keeping his eyes on Jack.

Elana, coming to her senses, pulled out her cellphone and snapped a quick picture of the criminal.

"I just sent a picture to you to the cops. You need to leave before they get here."

His eyes widened with this new knowledge, and he turned and ran away.

Shaking, she picked up Jack's leash and ran back to the van. Her grandmother was just coming out with a shopping bag.

"Guess what..." Grandma Cecilia saw the look on Elana's face and stopped in her tracks. "Elana, what happened? You're as pale as a sheet."

Elana fumbled with her keys to try to open the door. Jack was looking back at the park where they'd been, barking his head off. "Someone attacked me. We must leave."

Her grandmother's eyes widened. "Did he hurt you? Where is he? Did you call the police?"

She shook her head vehemently. "No. I just want to leave."

Her grandmother touched her arm. "Elana, did he hurt you?"

Elana investigated her grandmother's worried gaze. "He grabbed me, put his dirty hand over my mouth when I screamed. But Jack bit him, and he let me go." Hot tears slid down her face before she could control herself.

Grandma Cecilia looked truly horrified. "We need to tell the police."

Elana shook her head. "I don't want to stay here. I just want to leave. Please."

Her grandmother worried her lip with her teeth. Finally, she pulled her into her arms and held her tight. "Okay, we can leave. But I want to make a call to the police, so they are aware of this person."

Elana wiped her tears with the back of her hand. Jack sat at her feet and whined.

She bent and pulled the dog into a hug. "Thanks, Jack. You saved me."

Grandma Cecilia rubbed the dog between the ears. "You're getting a nice dinner tonight, Jack. Such a heroic animal."

Jack looked at her and let out a bark in agreement. This brought a smile to Elana's face.

"Let's go." Her grandmother opened the side of the van for Jack to get in.

Elana didn't need to be asked twice. She hurried into the driver's seat and slid in.

On their way out of town, Grandma Cecilia dialed the local police and informed them of the incident.

While they were disappointed that Elana didn't make a formal police report, they were grateful for the information and the photo that she had sent.

They had told her that the stranger's name was Paul Hudson, and he lived in the city. He'd been caught stalking a local girl who had a restraining order against him. He had a record for breaking and entering as well. They were going to pick him up for questioning.

Once they were on the interstate, Elana finally started feeling her anxiety ease.

As they drove, Jack rested his head on Elana's leg, refusing to leave her side.

CHAPTER 27

They pulled into West Yellowstone, Montana after dark. The small but charming town was picturesque.

"Which campground are we staying at?" She looked over at her grandmother.

"We're not staying at a campground tonight. I rented a proper cabin. I want to be fully rested before I see Ronald tomorrow." She squinted at her phone. "Take a left on this street. It should take you right there."

Elana wasn't going to argue. She welcomed a proper bed and hot shower, along with a secure door to lock out the danger of the outside world.

She followed Grandma Cecilia's directions. It was a line of cabins that backed along a dirt road.

"That's it up ahead." Her grandmother pointed. "The cabin with the blue door."

Elana eased the van into the small parking spot in front of the charming cabin and killed the engine. "We need to get settled into the cabin, and I'll start dinner."

Grandma Cecilia shook her head. "No need. Takeout is

on its way. I ordered it online when we rolled into town." She gave a grin.

"That sounds perfect. I'm starving and in need of a hot shower. I want to wash this whole day away."

Grandma Cecilia nodded. "You go on inside with the luggage. The password to the door lock is 1904."

Elana frowned. "But I need to walk Jack first."

Her grandmother shook her head. "I'll walk him. You go inside and get settled. Take a shower and get comfortable. By the time you're done, the food should be delivered."

Elana knew she should argue, but she was tired, physically and mentally. Instead, she gave her grandmother a grateful look and got out of the van to gather their clothes.

With her arms full of their clothing, she climbed the steps to the log cabin.

There was an Adirondack chair by the door, so she carefully laid the clothes over it so she could unlock the door.

Elana punched in the code and tried the doorknob. The door opened.

Gathering up her clothes, she walked inside and left the door ajar so her grandmother and Jack could get inside.

Laying the clothes on the blue and green plaid couch she walked through the cabin, taking in each room.

There was a small kitchen off the living room and a half bath down a hallway. One bedroom was situated on the main floor and had a full bath. The second bedroom was on the second floor with its own bathroom as well.

There was even a small reading nook off the balcony.

Jogging back downstairs, she smiled when Grandma Cecilia and Jack walked through the door.

"How's the cabin look, Elana?" her grandmother asked.

"Very cute. Two bedrooms. I can take the bedroom upstairs."

Grandma Cecilia smiled and nodded her head. "Okay.

Why don't you go get a shower, and I'll let you know when the food arrives?"

Elana nodded. "Sounds wonderful. I won't be long."

Her grandmother laughed. "Take your time."

Elana walked into the bedroom and grabbed some clean clothes. She'd already found the washer and dryer downstairs and planned on doing a load that night.

Heading into the bathroom, she turned to close the door. Jack was sitting in the doorway.

"I'm taking a shower, Jack."

When he didn't budge, she relented. "Come on in."

The dog stood, wagged his tail, and walked over to the bathmat in front of the shower, where he curled up.

She laughed.

Once the water got hot, she stepped inside and stood under the spray. She scrubbed every inch of her body, hoping to erase the memory of the day and the stench of the man who'd tried to assault her.

Hot unshed tears burned the back of her eyes, and she tried to blink them away unsuccessfully.

She finally lost the fight. Placing her hands on the walls of the shower, she sobbed.

And when she had let all her emotions out, she looked down. Jack was resting his head on the side of the shower, watching her, making sure she was okay.

Elana turned the water off. When she turned around, Jack had the towel in his mouth.

She quickly dried off and slipped on fresh clothes. She'd just finished drying her hair when she heard her grandmother.

"Food's here!" Grandma Cecilia called from downstairs.

Elana bent down and cuddled Jack in her arms. "Come on, Jack. Let's get something to eat."

CHAPTER 28

*E*lana finished off her meal by cracking open a fortune cookie. "That was the best Chinese food I have ever had."

Grandma Cecilia sighed with contentment. "I have to agree." She reached for a fortune cookie and then looked at Elana. "What does your fortune say?"

Elana tugged out the tiny scrap of paper and unrolled it. She frowned. "It says, 'The journey never ends.'"

Grandma Cecilia's face lit up. "That's very true, dear." She broke her cookie in half with excitement.

Elana studied her grandmother's face. "Well? Are you going to tell me what yours says?"

Grandma Cecilia slowly read her fortune. "'Don't fry bacon in the nude.'"

Elana blinked and burst out laughing. Her grandmother joined her, along with Jack letting out a bark while wagging his tail.

Elana collapsed back on the couch and smiled. "I needed that laugh." She glanced over at Jack. "Jack stayed in the bathroom with me and then handed me a towel when I got out of the shower."

Grandma Cecilia looked over at the canine, who was curled up in front of the fireplace. "Jack is a wise old dog. He's seen some things in life."

Elana snorted. "Grandma Cecilia, how do you know?"

She arched her brow. "I know things. Don't question me."

Elana grinned and nodded. "I think Jack is smart too. I'm beginning to think he found me instead of me finding him."

Her grandmother nodded. "That's how life is, honey. Nothing is by accident. It's like I've been telling you."

Elana heard her cell phone buzz again on the coffee table. When she saw it was from her father, she turned it off.

"I suppose that's your father again, checking up on me." Grandma Cecilia chewed thoughtfully on her cookie.

Elana frowned. "Yes. How did you know?"

She snorted. "I suspect he is wanting you to talk me into going into a nursing home. And he's keeping tabs on me, waiting on me to slip up and give him ammunition to gain total control of my money."

Elana shifted in her seat, uncomfortable at her grand-mother's statement. She didn't even have words to defend her father. How could she? What her grandmother said was true.

"I'm going to have a nice long soak in the tub before going to bed." Grandma Cecilia stood and stretched her arms over her head. "There is a fire pit on the back deck. You should start a fire and take a blanket with you to snuggle up. It's a perfect night for stargazing." She walked over to Elana and kissed her cheek. "Good night, dear."

She smiled. "Good night, Grandma Cecilia."

She watched her grandmother head to her room before turning to Jack. "Well, Jack. Do you feel up for a fire outside?"

Jack sat on his haunches and let out an affirming bark.

She grinned and grabbed her coat. Digging through the kitchen drawer, she pulled out a lighter. Her grandmother had bought a bottle of pinot noir that she had opened before she'd gone to have a bath.

Elana found a wineglass in a cabinet and poured herself a glass.

Grabbing the fuzzy throw on the back of the couch, she opened the back door to the deck.

Jack hurried over to the edge of the deck and looked around while she got busy making a fire.

She pulled a deck chair near the ring of fire and eased into the seat. She carefully wrapped the warm blanket over her before finally relaxing.

Elana took a sip of the wine and closed her eyes in bliss.

She opened her eyes and stared up at the starry night.

"It's beautiful," she said quietly. Jack rested his head on her thigh. She slowly petted the dog's head as she stared into the fire.

Her phone buzzed in her coat pocket.

Elana sighed and reached for it.

"Hello?"

"Elana, why haven't you called with an update? You should have made it to Montana yesterday." Her father's tone dripped with irritation.

She rolled her eyes. "We just made it."

He snorted. "Has she seen this man who is catfishing her?"

Elana shifted in her seat. "No. Tomorrow."

He chuckled. "She'll realize she made a big fool out of herself and come crawling back home. But that's okay. We'll take care of her when she gets home."

Elana gritted her teeth. "I don't think Grandma Cecilia needs anyone to take care of her."

Her father barked out a laugh. "Are you crazy? After this

stunt she pulled? She's lucky she'll even be granted an allowance after this."

Elana felt her whole body go hot with rage. "Careful, Father. You wouldn't want Grandma Cecilia to realize how cruel her son turned out to be. A son who only wants to put her in a nursing home so he can get her money."

He stuttered on the other end of the line, clearly shocked that Elana had stood up for her grandmother.

He started to offer some kind of apology, but she didn't want to hear it.

"I've got to go. Tomorrow is a busy day." She ended the call and put her phone away.

He called back, and she turned her phone off.

Leaning back in the chair, she stared up at the sky.

"Is it wrong to dread going back home after this trip is over, Jack?"

The canine lifted his head and cocked an ear.

"It's only been a few days, but it feels like it's been weeks since we were back in South Carolina. But now, I'm not ready for this trip to end."

Jack whined and laid his head on her thigh.

"Am I missing out on how life should be lived because I'm so scared to try something out of the ordinary?" She looked at Jack.

"Did you know I wanted to be an artist when I was younger. I used to love drawing flowers and animals in elementary school. I wanted to do that instead of dance, but my mother insisted that there was no future in art." She sighed. "I've lived my life by the expectations of others."

Her grandmother had done the same, yet here she was, starting her own life on her own terms.

The thing was, Elana didn't want to wait until she was old to live.

Something had to give.
And someone was going to be disappointed.
She just hoped it wasn't her.

CHAPTER 29

"Come on, we're going to be late." Elana took the last sip of her coffee before rinsing her coffee mug and placing it in the dishwasher.

Grandma Cecilia had rented the cabin for the next few days since she was unsure of what was going to happen.

"I'm coming," Grandma Cecilia called out from her bedroom. She appeared in the kitchen dressed to kill in black jeans, black cowboy boots, and a pretty cornflower-blue blouse. She held up a cowboy hat. "Will it be too much if I wear the hat?" She gave Elana an uncertain look.

"Take it. You might want to wear it once you get there." She walked over and took her grandmother's hands into hers. "You look beautiful."

Grandma Cecilia's face lit up. "You think so?"

She nodded. "Absolutely. And if he thinks otherwise, then he's an idiot. And I know you don't tolerate idiots."

This brought a smile to her face. "You're right. Is Jack ready?"

Elana nodded. "He's been fed and walked. We are just waiting on you."

Her grandmother gathered her purse. "Let's hit the road. Ronald offered to meet us here to take us to the ranch, but I insisted on driving over there myself. That way we can leave when we are ready."

Elana slid her coat on and picked up the van keys. "Good idea. You have the directions, right?"

Her grandmother showed her the directions on her phone. "Not far from here."

They walked out of the cabin, and Elana locked up behind them. Grandma Cecilia had beat her to the van and was waiting impatiently for her to unlock the door.

She couldn't help but grin. Seeing her grandmother look so happy and excited was a wonderful thing. She deserved it.

After they all climbed into the van, Elana backed out of the driveway and followed the directions to Ronald's farm.

She glanced over at her grandmother. "What if he's different than what you expected?"

The older woman shrugged. "We all age, Elana. He's not going to look the same."

Elana nodded. "I know, but what if once you meet in person, you feel differently about him?"

Grandma Cecilia stared at her.

Elana shook her head slowly. "I just don't want you to be disappointed. That's all."

Her grandmother reached over and squeezed her arm. "Disappointed? Never. I would be disappointed if I hadn't come out here." She smiled and laid her head against the seat.

Elana envied her grandmother. She wanted to be as brave as she was. To follow her heart and throw caution to wind was something Elana had never done.

"Turn up ahead, dear." Her grandmother pointed at a driveway ahead.

She slowed the VW van and made the turn into the driveway.

Elana squinted to see the faded name on the mailbox but couldn't make out the letters. Trusting her grandmother to get them where they needed to go, she slowly drove up the driveway.

They approached a small white house with a porch. The paint was peeling, and a shutter was hanging at an angle.

Her stomach sank. Maybe this guy really was after Grandma Cecilia's money.

She stopped in front of the house and put the van in Park. She looked over at her grandmother. "Are you sure this is the place? Want me to knock on the door and make sure we're at the right house?"

Her grandmother worried her lip with her teeth. She slowly shook her head. "No, I'll go. It was my idea to come here, so I'll go knock on the door." She pulled out a compact mirror from her purse and checked her appearance one last time. She gave Elana a tight smile and then opened the door.

Elana watched her grandmother approach the house. The van was silent except for the sound of Jack's panting near her ear. She looked at the dog. He licked the side of her face and kept watching Grandma Cecilia.

Her grandmother knocked, and then the door opened slightly. Elana leaned forward to get a look but couldn't see anything in the shadow.

Grandma Cecilia spoke to someone and then turned and headed back to the van. As soon as she opened the door, Elana leaned forward.

"Is he here? Did you speak to him?"

Grandma Cecilia shook her head. "That was the house-keeper, Hattie. This is her house. Ronald's house is farther up the road." She pointed at a dirt road running alongside of the house. "Go down that road. It should take you to the main house."

Elana started the car. "The main house. So, Ronald has a separate house for the housekeeper?"

Grandma sighed heavily. "She's the cook too. And to answer your question, yes, Ronald has a separate house for the housecleaner."

Elana cut her eyes at her. "Is she young?"

Grandma Cecilia snorted. "She's older than me. Said she's been with the family since she was young."

Elana droves slowly up the driveway. "So, she's not as pretty as you?"

Grandma Cecilia turned to Elana and blinked. "She doesn't have a tooth in her head. Does that answer your question?"

Elana snorted and then bit back a laugh. "It does."

The rest of the drive was silent. The tension in the van was palpable. Even Jack was perched between them, panting heavily waiting for the house to come into view.

Just then, the house appeared over a hill.

"Just like I imagined," Grandma Cecilia breathed.

Elana gaped at the sprawling ranch house. It was built of stone and logs and looked like something out of a movie.

"You said he was a rancher?" She pulled up to the house and killed the engine.

"A cattle rancher."

Elana looked at her grandmother with wide eyes. "I guess the ranching business is booming."

Her grandmother cracked a smile. "You could say that."

Elana looked back at the massive house. The large front door opened, and a tall older man stepped out on to the porch. He was dressed all in black, including his cowboy hat.

Grandma Cecilia gasped.

She jerked her head in her grandmother's direction. "Is that him, Grandma Cecilia?"

Her grandmother said nothing. She reached for the handle and opened the door. She slowly got out of the van.

Jack jumped into her vacant seat and looked over at Elana.

Grandma Cecilia shut the van door behind her.

"We'll stay here and give her some privacy," she said to the dog.

Jack seemed to understand, and they both sat watching her grandmother.

The man walked off the porch and grinned when he saw her grandmother. He quickly closed the distance between them and picked her up in a big bear hug.

She buried her face in his neck as they held each other tightly.

Elana felt her face burn with embarrassment at watching the intimate moment between former lovers.

She glanced at Jack and blinked.

"Elana, come on out. I want you to meet someone," her grandmother called out.

She looked up and saw her grandmother looking happier than she'd ever seen her, her arms wrapped around this man's waist.

Elana grabbed Jack's leash and secured the dog before opening the van door.

Jack did his business on a nearby oak tree before he was ready to walk.

Elana smiled as she approached the man. "Hello, I'm Elana."

The man smiled broadly, took off hat, and stuck out his hand. "I'm Ronald. And I already know who you are, Elana. Your grandmother speaks very highly of you."

Elana didn't cringe under his calloused hand. Instead, she gave him a warm smile. "And my grandmother has told me nothing about you. Until recently."

Ronald barked out a laugh. "I bet. That sounds like Cecilia. Always keeping things close to the vest. I'm glad you two made it here okay. You can imagine my surprise when she told me you two were going to drive to Montana instead of flying."

Grandma Cecilia arched her brow. "If I was going to make this long journey, I was going to make it in the VW." She nodded to the van.

Ronald looked at the van and shook his head. "I can't believe you came all the way in that thing." He looked back at Elana. "When we found each other online, Cecilia told me about this old van. Said she originally bought it so she could travel and see America."

Grandma Cecilia rested her head on his shoulder and sighed. "But work quickly took over my life, leaving no room for travel. But I kept it, thinking one day I could make my dream come true. And it's done more than that. It brought me back to you, Ronald." She looked up at him with stars in her eyes.

"That's right, darling." He smiled down at her.

Jack barked, catching everyone's attention.

Ronald laughed. "You didn't say you were bringing your dog."

Cecilia shook her head. "That's not Winston. That's Jack, Elana's dog. We picked him up at the dog rescue in Mississippi. He's turned out to be not only a good traveling companion but good protection as well."

Elana swallowed back the memory of yesterday. She cleared her throat. "So, this is all your land, Ronald?"

He nodded and put his hand on his head. "Yes ma'am. Inherited some of it from my uncle since he didn't have any children. Over the years I've continued to buy more land and add more cattle." He looked over the land with the mountains in the backdrop.

"It's beautiful. I've never been to Montana, but it's certainly breathtaking," Elana added.

"I'm glad you approve, Elana. Now why don't both of you come inside and have some homemade apple pie. Hattie made it from scratch yesterday before she went home for the weekend." Ronald turned toward the house.

"That sounds wonderful." Grandma Cecilia linked her arm through his.

Elana glanced down at Jack. "What about Jack? Is he allowed inside?"

Ronald nodded enthusiastically. "Of course. He can play with Nelson, my yellow lab."

They walked across the yard toward the house.

Elana swallowed as she took the first step up to the massive front porch.

Maybe her grandmother was right. Maybe anything was possible if you just believed hard enough.

CHAPTER 30

*E*lana forked the last bite of apple pie into her mouth and sighed. "Tell Hattie that was the best apple pie I have ever eaten." She finished it off with a sip of hot coffee.

She looked over at the fireplace where Jack had made friends with Nelson. They were lying side by side playing tug-of-war with an old bone.

Ronald nodded. "I will do that. She has today and tomorrow off, but she'll be back after that. We're having a large dinner, and she is cooking. I want to introduce you both to my ranch hands."

Grandma Cecilia beamed. "That sounds wonderful. And we will help Hattie, so all that work won't fall on her shoulders."

Ronald snorted. "You can offer, but Hattie prefers to have the kitchen all to herself She's been cooking for me for years now and is pretty set in her ways."

Elana laughed. "Sounds very strong-willed. Much like someone I know." She cut her eyes at her grandmother, who shot her a look.

"Let's get your stuff inside and I'll show you to your rooms. Then I'll give you the tour of the land."

Grandma Cecilia looked at Elana. Ronald caught their exchange.

He narrowed his eyes slightly. "I just assumed you'd both be staying here."

Grandma Cecilia cleared her throat. "I rented the cabin for a few more days. I thought Elana would enjoy some time to herself since she had been stuck in a van with me for nearly a week."

Elana bit back a smile. She knew what her grandmother was doing. She was the one who wanted privacy. She wanted to be alone with Ronald.

Who could blame her?

"I hope you don't mind. I was going to spend the night at the cabin with Jack," Elana stated, backing up her grandmother.

"Of course not." He blushed a little when he looked at her grandmother. "This will give me and Cecilia time to catch up."

Elana looked away. She hoped that talking was all they were going to do.

She stood and carried her plate to the sink. "I'll go grab your things, Grandma Cecilia."

Ronald shook her head. "I'll get it. I insist."

Grandma Cecilia stood and nodded. "I'll go with you. Ronald, you don't mind if Elana takes a tour of the house?"

He smiled broadly. "Of course not. Have a look around, Elana. We'll be back shortly."

Elana watched the couple head outside. She ran over to the window just in time to see Ronald reaching out to hold her grandmother's hand.

Her heart melted at the sight.

She turned away to give the couple some privacy.

Looking around the massive kitchen, she decided to take Ronald up on his offer and walked around the house.

The living room had an open plan with a large stone fireplace. Picture windows on either side provided magnificent views of the mountains. Large moose antlers hung above the fireplace, and there were some pictures placed along the mantel.

She pictured up a frame photo and studied the group of men victoriously posing in front of a large downed moose. Setting the picture back on the mantel, she decided to make her way upstairs.

The stairs were as massive as the rest of the house. Black-and-white framed photos of wild animals lined the walls leading up the stairs.

Reaching the top, she walked down a hallway and stopped at a room. Elana stepped inside the large bedroom. Again, it was beautifully decorated, but there wasn't anything personal like pictures on the wall.

She went through all the rooms upstairs until she came to the master bedroom. Stepping inside, she saw this room was more personal than the others.

The large king-size bed was decorated in cool gray colors, and along the fireplace were pictures of Ronald when he was younger. Stepping closer, Elana realized all the photos were pictures of Ronald and her grandmother.

Picking up a photo, she marveled that he'd kept the photos all these years.

"I always carried a photo of Cecilia with me."

Elana jumped at Ronald's voice and spun around.

"Sorry, I didn't mean to frighten you."

She smiled and shook her head. "I should be the one apologizing to you. I had no business in your room." She looked past him. "Where's Grandma Cecilia?"

He grinned. "She's sitting on the porch and enjoying the view."

Elana smiled. "You do have fantastic views."

He walked over to the window, shoved his hands in his jeans pocket, and stared out. "I'm sure you have a ton of questions for me." He threw a look at her over his shoulder.

"What kind of granddaughter would I be if I didn't?" she joked.

He turned and studied her. "You know, your grandmother values your opinion over everyone else's in the family."

Elana blinked, caught off guard.

He grinned. "You didn't know that. Why don't we go outside with your grandmother." He walked over to the doorway and waited for her to exit first.

As she descended the stairs, she pointed to the pictures on the wall. "Are these from your hunts?"

"Some are. Some are just photos I've taken on vacation." He stopped at a picture of a huge bear. "I took this photo on a bear hunt in Alaska."

She looked at him. "Did you shoot him?"

He slowly shook his head. "No, I didn't. Once I saw how huge he was, I decided to let him live another day. Now if he had been an elk, he would have been a goner."

She reached the bottom step. "I like your house. It's beautiful. Seems like there's a lot of history in these walls."

He nodded and walked over to the front door. Jack and Nelson hopped up from where they were lounging at the fireplace and ran over. "It's been in my family for a while. Every generation has either improved the house or added to it." He opened the door and waited for her to walk out. Jack and Nelson raced past her.

"There you two are. I was wondering what was taking you so long. You didn't get lost, did you, Elana?" Grandma Cecilia joked.

"Just taking my time looking at Ronald's beautiful house," Elana assured her.

"Come sit." Grandma Cecilia eased over on the wicker couch and patted her hand on the seat.

Elana sat next to her. Ronald sat in the chair next to her grandmother.

"This is more beautiful than I imagined, Ronald." Grandma Cecilia looked over at him. "I bet you have coffee out here every morning just to take in the view."

He took her hand in his and grinned. "I get up before the sun comes up, Cecilia. But I do have an evening cocktail out here." He chuckled.

"Even better," Grandma Cecilia stated.

Elana stood and walked over to the edge of the porch. "How many cattle do you have?"

"About six thousand."

Elana felt her eyes go wide. "That's a lot."

He shrugged. "It was more, but I sold some back in the spring. I'll buy more next year."

Elana nodded. "Sounds like business is good."

Ronald looked at her. "I can't complain."

Jack and Nelson wandered off the porch into the front yard. Elana frowned and watched the dogs walk behind the house.

"Don't worry. Nelson is probably showing Jack her bone yard." Ronald grinned.

Elana grimaced. "Bone yard?"

He chuckled. "Nelson digs a hole and puts his bones in the backyard. He saves them for a rainy day, I suppose."

Elana shrugged. She wasn't sure Jack wasn't going to run off, so she bounded down the steps. "I'll just make sure they're okay."

She didn't wait for Ronald to reassure her but instead hurried around the house.

When she got to the back of the house, she was surprised to find a pretty flower garden.

The summer flowers had grown brown, but there were a few late bloomers still filling some of the raised beds with flowers. She examined it more closely and noticed there was a sign sticking out of the ground. *Cecilia's flowers.*

Ronald had planted Grandma Cecilia her own flower garden since he knew her love of flowers.

She laughed to herself. Ronald was certainly a more complicated man than she'd thought.

Elana glanced around for Jack.

She spotted him with Nelson under a tree. He was watching Nelson intently as the dog dug a hole. When he popped his head out of the hole, he was holding a bone.

Elana shoved her hands in her coat pocket and walked past the backyard.

Ronald didn't have a fence, so the backyard opened up to a large rolling pasture with mountains in the background. It looked like something in a picture.

"Elana, we are going to get a tour of the farm," Grandma Cecilia called out.

"Coming." She patted her leg, and Jack ran over to her. Both dogs followed her around the house to the front of the yard.

Ronald was holding the passenger-side door of his large Ram truck open for her grandmother. She walked over and opened the back door.

She started to get in but stopped. "Ronald, do you mind if Jack rides back here?"

He shut her grandmother's door and let out a laugh. "I would be offended if he didn't. Why, Nelson rides everywhere with me."

Elana relaxed and called Jack up into the truck. Nelson

waited until Ronald gave the command and jumped in the back seat with them.

Elana watched as Ronald walked around the hood of the truck.

"What do you think of him, Elana?" Grandma Cecilia whispered.

Elana grinned. "I think I can see why you've fallen in love."

Her grandmother turned in her seat and reached for her hand. Taking Elana's hand in hers, she gave her a squeeze.

Ronald climbed in the truck and gave them an amused look. "I'm guessing you two were talking about me."

Grandma Cecilia lifted her chin and smirked. "It's girl talk. None of your business."

He chuckled and started the engine.

As they pulled out of the driveway, Elana gazed upon the massive land that might be her grandmother's new home.

CHAPTER 31

*E*lana stuck her head out of the window as Ronald gave them the tour of his ranch. They didn't have to drive far before she began to see cattle.

A group of cowboys were herding the cattle to the east, and even Jack let out an excited bark when he spotted them.

"Sounds like Jack likes cattle," Ronald joked. "I bet he would make a great cattle dog and help herd."

Elana grinned. "I don't know about that. Maybe in his youth. He has some age on him now. But he seems to have been a little more active since we started heading into the mountains. What do you think, Grandma Cecilia?"

Her grandmother turned in her seat to look at her. "Jack seems like a different dog now. I think it's the mountain air. Or maybe he just likes to travel."

Jack put his paws on the console and gave her grandmother a lick on the face. She let out a laugh.

"How old is Jack?"

Elana shrugged. "I don't remember Ethan telling us. I'm guessing nine or ten. His owner was an older gentleman who was put in a nursing home. Jack went to the dog rescue."

Ronald reached over and petted the dog. Jack nuzzled his hand.

Jack approved of Ronald. To Elana, that was a good sign.

"Jack is also very protective of Elana. Why, just yesterday he saved Elana from a potential kidnapping," Grandma Cecilia stated.

Elana closed her eyes. "Grandma Cecilia. I don't want to talk about that."

Ronald brows furrowed. "Tell me you have a gun to protect yourselves."

Grandma Cecilia shrugged. "Didn't think I needed one. I mean, Jack tore into that guy who grabbed Elana."

Ronald looked horrified. Elana was humiliated.

"Did you two go to the police? Make a report?" Ronald asked.

Elana shook her head. "No. I didn't want to. When he grabbed me, Jack jumped on him and bit him until he let me go. After that, we left. I didn't want to stay there anymore."

Ronald nodded. "That's understandable. I'm glad you had Jack with you. But you need to think about something else for protection. Even if it's just bear spray."

Her grandmother chuckled. "We don't have bear spray in South Carolina."

Ronald nodded. "Bear spray is better than pepper spray. Elana, I'll get you some for your trip home."

Elana nodded.

"Now, let's talk about something more pleasant. Have you camped out on a ranch before?" Ronald asked.

Elana was relieved he had changed the subject.

"Actually, we have. A rancher in Wyoming was kind enough to let us spend the night after we had a flat. We ate with the ranch hands and slept in the van." Grandma Cecilia grinned.

Ronald studied her for a second. "I don't suppose it would be Dennis McClintock, would it?"

Her grandmother brightened. "How did you know?"

He snorted. "Dennis is an old friend of mine. And he has a large ranch as well. Not big as mine, but pretty big."

Grandma Cecilia arched a brow. "You don't seem jealous, Ronald. Dennis could have swept me off my feet."

Ronald grinned. "I know Dennis. He has a serious girlfriend. And he knows better than to step out on her. Flora would cook his goose if he ever tried something."

Elana let out a laugh. "He was a perfect gentleman. He also stopped when we had a flat."

Ronald nodded. "I'll have to thank him for that." He reached over and took her grandmother's hand in his. He gently kissed the back of her hand.

Elana felt her face heat at the intimate moment. She quickly turned her attention out the window. Jack let out a bark and climbed in her lap. Looking out the window, he began to whine.

"I think he has to do his business," Ronald stated.

Elana frowned. "Do you think he'll be okay if I let him out? I don't want him to frighten the cattle."

Ronald chuckled. "I have a feeling he'll be fine. We'll all get out and stretch our legs."

He opened his door and climbed out.

Jack looked at her and barked.

"Fine, Jack, but don't run off. I don't know what I'd do if I lost you."

The dog stared in her eyes and then licked her from chin to forehead.

She laughed and wiped the kiss off with the back of her hand. "Let's go." She reached for the handle and opened the door.

Jack jumped out of the truck before she could climb out. He ran about twenty feet, stopped, and relieved himself.

Zipping up her jacket, she walked over to him, and they stood watching the cowboys drive the cattle on.

CHAPTER 32

Jack lifted his face to the breeze. This was what he loved best. The scent of the mountain air, the cows, and the impending snow.

He looked back at Elana. She looked worried. She thought he was going to run off.

He wondered why she was always so worried about what happened next.

He wished he could tell her that life was a continual journey. Every day was a new starting point. Where you wanted to end up usually came with a lot of detours and stumbling blocks. But that was part of the adventure.

He looked back at a cow who had strayed from the herd.

The cowboys were busy and had missed seeing her. They were almost over the ridge, and once they were out of eyesight, they would move on without her.

His instincts kicked in. He had to do something. He raced over in the cow's direction.

He could hear Elana screaming behind him to come back, but he was on a mission.

He ran over to the cow, who lowered her head. He let out

a bark to tell her to turn back to the rest of the cattle. But she was an ornery one. She mooed that she wasn't going to let him tell her what to do.

Baring his teeth, he growled and then let out another bark.

The cow batted her lashes and then finally turned back in the direction the cattle were heading.

One of the cowboys heard his bark and looked back. Eyes wide, he turned his horse toward them and began herding the stray back to the herd.

The cowboy looked at Jack, tipped his hat and said, "Thank you."

Jack sat and watched.

Elana ran over to him and dropped to her knees beside him. "Jack. I thought you were going to run off." She wrapped her arms around his neck and hugged him tight.

Suddenly, Grandma Cecilia and Ronald were there with big smiles on their faces.

"I told you he was a cow dog. Good job, Jack." Ronald rubbed his head.

"Such a smart dog, Jack." Grandma Cecilia clasped her hands together as she praised him.

He looked over at Elana. She swallowed hard and nodded. "Yes, you are a good dog, Jack."

He gave her a toothy smile. And then licked her from chin to forehead.

This time she didn't wipe his kiss off.

CHAPTER 33

*A*fter getting the tour from Ronald, Elana asked if she could walk back to the house instead of ride. She wanted some time to herself and said that Jack could keep her company.

Before Grandma Cecilia and Ronald pulled away, Elana fished her cell phone out of her coat pocket and tossed it on the back seat of the truck.

Since they had arrived, her cell phone had been buzzing with missed calls from her father.

She didn't want to talk to him right now. She wanted time alone to think.

Her grandmother had handed her a small notebook and pencil. She said she might want to put her artistic talent to the test and sketch some of her surroundings.

As they drove away, she glanced down at Jack and then at the leash in her hand.

"I don't suppose you need this." She wrapped up the leash and shoved it in her pocket.

"Let's have a nice walk, just you and me."

Jack looked up at her and cocked his head as if he understood exactly what she was saying.

Elana stuck her hands in her pocket and started to walk in the direction of the house. She took her time, taking in the scent of mountain air and the way the dying grass would wave in the wind.

She glanced over at the mountain range. She'd never seen anything so beautiful in her whole life.

Stopping, she reached for the unlined notepad and pencil in her pocket. Sinking down, she sat on the ground. Jack sat beside her and watched as she began to sketch the mountains.

Elana took her time, wanting to make sure she captured the essence and the magic of the natural wonder.

Jack's head jerked up. He spotted something a few yards away. She watched as a prairie dog popped its head out of hole.

Jack slowly stood and began easing his way over to the prairie dog.

Elana grinned and quickly turned the page of the notebook. She began drawing the scene in front of her.

The prairie dog let out a string of chatter, and Jack barked and leapt on the hole. The prairie dog disappeared before Jack could catch it.

But Jack was not deterred. He began digging in the hole, trying to ferret the animal out.

"Jack, come on." Elana stood and dusted off her jeans. She stuck her notepad and pencil back in her coat and waited for Jack to join her.

The dog finally lifted his dirt-filled nose out of the hole and stared at her.

"Come on, boy. Let's go back to the house. I bet Nelson has a bone he'll share with you."

Jack's ears stood at attention, and he jogged over to her.

"Sometimes I think you know exactly what I'm saying, Jack." She rubbed the canine between the ears.

They walked in silence back to the house. She hadn't felt that at peace in forever.

Smiling she stepped onto the porch just as her grandmother came running out the front door.

"I've been trying to call you, Elana. You didn't answer."

She cringed. "I left my phone in the truck. Sorry about that. Is everything okay?"

Grandma Cecilia shook her head. "No. Your father called me. He said since you've been ignoring his calls, he wanted to let me know that he was on his way here."

Elana froze. "Father is coming to Montana?"

She slowly nodded her head. "And he's bringing his attorney with him. To make me sign the papers to be committed to a nursing home."

Elana felt the blood drain from her face. "He can't force you into doing that. It's not legal."

Sadness and desperation etched into her grandmother's face. "He said that I'm mentally unable to care for myself. And that he's doing this for my own good. I can't believe my own son is doing this to me. I don't even recognize him anymore."

Elana's fingers tightened into fists. "It's not right. None of this is right."

Her grandmother turned and headed back into the house, looking like a defeated woman.

Elana turned and ran to the truck. Opening the back door, she grabbed her phone.

She listened to every missed call from her father. He said he was on his way to Montana to settle things once and for all.

Elana let out a frustrated scream which made Jack bark.

She looked down at her dog. "I can't let this happen, Jack. This will destroy her."

Jack cocked his head and stared at her.

Steeling her resolve, she marched back into the house.

CHAPTER 34

Grandma Cecilia had locked herself in the upstairs bedroom, refusing to talk to Elana. She would only allow Ronald to come in the room.

Sitting by the door, she jumped up when Ronald came out. "I need to talk to her," Elana insisted.

Ronald shook his head slowly. "I'm afraid Cecilia is too upset to talk. She looks so worried." Ronald narrowed his eyes. "If her son thinks he's going to come into my house and take Cecilia away from me, he's got another thing coming."

Elana shook her head. "I can't believe he thinks he can do this. This is his own mother." Elana swallowed. "When Father found out I was going on this trip with Grandma Cecilia, he was okay with it. He told me that once she got here, she would realize that she had been catfished by someone who only wanted her money. That's why he thinks he is protecting her. It must be."

Ronald snorted. "Elana, you have a good heart. But I'm afraid your father isn't telling you everything."

Elana stilled. The hair on the back of her neck stood up. "What do you mean?"

Ronald gritted his teeth. "I promised Cecilia I wouldn't say a thing. This is her business to tell. But I will say this. I've asked Cecilia to marry me, and she said yes. She's not going back to South Carolina." He gave her one last look and headed down the stairs.

Elana slid down the wall. She wasn't sure she could handle one more piece of news. Her phone buzzed in her pocket. She dug it out and saw a text from her father stating he would be in Montana tonight. She rested her head against the wall.

Jack came bounding up the stairs with a stick in his mouth. He set it at Elana's feet.

She bent and picked it up. "I can't play fetch with you right now, Jack. We have a serious situation going on."

Jack sat and stared at the stick in her hand. Sighing she patted her leg. "Come on. Let's go outside." She headed down the stairs with Jack beside her.

Ronald was standing at the fireplace, resting one arm on the mantel and staring down into the flames.

"Father sent a text. He'll be here tonight."

Ronald looked over at her. "If that man steps one foot on my property, I'll shoot him."

Elana cocked her head. "I don't think the police will let you get away with that."

He arched a brow. "Who said I would call the police?"

Elana shook her head. "Look, don't do anything crazy. Give me some time to talk some sense into him. Once I talk to him and allay his fears that Grandma Cecilia is of sound mind and body, he'll relent."

Ronald shook his head. "I love your optimism, Elana. But I've lived a lot longer than you. And you are putting your hope in the wrong person."

Elana sighed. "I'm not giving up. Not yet."

He gave her a nod.

"I'm going to head back to the cabin with Jack. I need some time to think."

Ronald shoved away from the mantel. "Do you want me or one of my men to follow you and make sure you get there safe? I know you must be shaken up after what happened."

She smiled. "No. That's okay. I have Jack. But I appreciate the offer."

He nodded.

She looked down at her dog. "Come on, Jack. Let's go."

CHAPTER 35

*E*lana took a long shower when she got back to the cabin. Just like before, Jack sat on the bathmat and waited for her.

She put on a black sweater and black jeans. It was the dressiest thing she had brought. Her father wouldn't approve, but frankly, she didn't care. She was more concerned about her grandmother's well-being.

She grabbed her coat and reached inside the pocket to retrieve her gloves. Her hand brushed against the notepad.

She pulled it out and sat down on the couch.

Elana looked back at the sketch of the mountain and cocked her head. Grabbing her pencil, she filled in some areas. When she was done, she turned the page.

"Look, Jack. That's you." She held out the sketch of the dog digging in the prairie dog hole. "I'll have to show Grandma Cecilia."

Jack let out a sharp bark.

Elana stood and slipped her coat on. She knew it was time to head back to Ronald's ranch, and she grabbed her keys.

She loaded Jack up in the VW before getting behind the wheel. They drove in silence.

When she pulled up to the house, she spotted an unfamiliar black SUV.

Elana's stomach sank.

Her father had arrived.

Steeling herself, she stepped out of the van. Jack jumped down from the seat and landed on the ground. He looked up at her.

"I guess it's now or never, Jack."

Jack barked.

She grinned.

Elana walked across the yard toward the massive house. Before she reached the first step leading up to the porch, the front door opened.

Her father stepped out, dressed in a three-piece suit. He frowned when he saw her.

"Father. How was your trip?" She climbed the steps.

Her father crossed his arms. "Long. Elana, why are you dressed like that? I would have expected you to dress up for my arrival."

She blinked. For the first time in her life, she really listened to her father's words. Then she burst out laughing.

He uncrossed his arms and stared at her like she had lost her mind. "What has gotten into you? What's so funny?"

She shook her head and composed herself. "You are. We are on a ranch, Father. Why would I wear a cocktail dress on a ranch? That's utterly ridiculous."

He looked quite offended, but for once she didn't care.

She walked past him and stepped into the house with Jack at her side.

Ronald stood there at the fireplace with a glare etched into his face. Elana could tell it was taking all his restraint not to throttle her father.

"Hi, Elana," Ronald said but kept his gaze narrowed on her father.

"Where's Grandma Cecilia?" she asked.

"She's upstairs in her room."

Her father snorted. "Her room? This isn't her home."

Ronald curled his fingers into fists. "This is Cecilia's home for as long as she wants."

Elana walked over to Ronald and nodded. She turned to face her father. "So why did you come all the way here, Father?"

He lifted his chin in the air. "When you stopped answering my calls, I got concerned. Grandma has been away from home too long. I came to put an end to this nonsense and bring her home."

She blinked. "You mean you came to take her to the assisted living home." She waited for his reaction. To his credit, he gave none.

"Your grandmother needs a place that takes proper care of her. It's clear that she is making irrational decisions," her father stated.

In that moment, she lost a lot of respect for her father. In that moment, he felt like a stranger to her.

"I don't need any such thing," Grandma Cecilia called down from the top of the staircase.

Everyone turned.

Grandma Cecilia was dressed in a sapphire blue pantsuit, her hair and makeup perfectly done.

She looked years younger. But there was one thing that was the same. The determination in her eyes.

Slowly, she descended the staircase, looking like a goddess.

Elana had seen that look on her grandmother's face many times before when she was making business deals.

Elana bit back a grin.

"John Taylor, there was no need for you to travel all the way to Montana. You've wasted your time." Grandma Cecilia reached the bottom step and glared at her son.

Her father lifted his chin. "Mother, this has gone on long enough. I was generous enough to allow you to travel across the States on this fool's errand. But it stops now. I've brought my attorney, Mr. Collins, who has the legal documents for you to sign."

Elana held her breath. She expected her grandmother to fly across the room in a rage and slap the crap out of her father. Instead, she only grinned and walked over to Ronald.

She slipped her hand in his.

"I won't be signing any documents, John. Not today or any other day." She smirked.

Suddenly the front door swung open, and a man wearing a suit and carrying a briefcase sauntered in.

"Who the hell are you?" Ronald thundered.

"I'm Mr. Collins. I believe I'm here on business with Mrs. Cecilia Taylor." He smoothed down his Hermès tie.

"I am Mrs. Cecilia Taylor and I have no business with you. So, Mr. Collins, you can leave." She snorted.

Her father pressed his lips into a thin line and glared at Elana. "Now is the time for you to speak up, Elana. You're only hurting your grandmother by going along with her charade."

Elana held her father's gaze. "I'm confused as to what you think I'm supposed to do. Grandma Cecilia is an adult and is fully capable of caring her herself. I don't see any need for her to go to an assisted living."

Her father's face shifted into something dark. "Elana, you forget yourself. I know you have been trying to get a raise at your job. Your boss and I are on friendly terms, and I can see that it happens."

Elana felt her face heat with anger. She clenched her jaw

to keep the overwhelming outrage from spilling out into the room.

The room fell silent.

Mr. Collins cleared his throat and stepped forward.

Ronald narrowed his eyes on the lawyer. "I don't remember inviting you in. In Montana, uninvited guests are dealt with harshly."

Mr. Collins's eyes widened, and he took a step back. "But Mr. Taylor assured me…"

Elana had had enough. She stepped forward. "Mr. Collins, you are here under false assumptions. My grandmother is of sound mind and body, and no one here is signing any papers to put her in a nursing home."

He shifted his weight. "Assisted living. But your father said this is in her best interest."

Elana lifted her chin. "My father is mistaken. And if you try to push this any further, then I'm afraid I'll have to see legal advice myself to see what can be done to a person who falsely imprisons someone in a nursing home. I'll see to it that not only will you lose your license, you'll get prison time as well. I don't think you are the kind of man that will do well in prison."

This got his attention. Mr. Collins gave her father a look and then grabbed his briefcase and exited the door.

"Elana, you will regret what you've just done," her father thundered at her. He took a step toward her, but Jack intervened. He showed his teeth and growled menacingly at him.

Her father's eyes widened. Despite his fear, he stood his ground. "You don't understand. She is giving all her money to this man. There will be nothing left for me. I need her money."

Elana's mouth dropped. She glanced over at Grandma Cecilia and then back at her father.

Grandma Cecilia stepped forward and stood by Elana. "I

knew this was about money all along. Elana, I'm afraid your father hasn't been honest with you."

Elana swallowed. "What do you mean?"

Ronald walked over to the side table and poured himself a bourbon. "I think your father should tell you, but he's too much of a coward."

Elana glared at her father. "What is he talking about?"

He lifted his chin and looked away.

Her grandmother took her hand in hers and patted it. "Your father wants me to go to the nursing home so he can have total control of my money. You see, dear, he's so far in debt he'll never get out."

Elana gasped and placed a hand over her mouth. "Is that true?" She stared at her father.

He looked away.

"It's true, Elana." Her grandmother squeezed her hand. "About three months ago, he came to me asking me to sign over control of the company. He said it was time for me to retire and enjoy life. Knowing your father, I decided to have my attorney to investigate his finances. Turns out he's basically broke and wanted control of my money so they won't foreclose on his house."

Elana stared at her father. "What do you have to say for yourself?"

He ran a finger around the neck of his shirt. "It's a little more complicated."

Her grandmother nodded. "It seems he's also being blackmailed by the twenty-three-year-old girl in his office that he's been sleeping with."

Her father looked away.

Elana glared. "You're cheating on Mother?"

He sighed and looked away. "My marriage is not any of your concern."

Grandma Cecilia sighed. "Once I realized what was going

on, I opened up an account here in Montana and started moving my money here. Away from your father."

Elana glared at her father. "How could you?"

He lifted his chin and glanced away, refusing to answer.

Elana swallowed hard and started for the door.

"Where are you going?" her father demanded.

"I need some fresh air. It seems like the family I thought I knew was an illusion." She patted her leg for Jack, who followed her outside.

CHAPTER 36

*E*lana stormed out the door onto the front porch. She bounced down the steps with Jack on her heels.

She passed close to the SUV her father had arrived in and saw Mr. Collins sitting in the passenger seat talking on his cell phone.

Elana changed her mind. Instead of heading to the VW van, she changed direction and headed to the backyard. She didn't stop but continued walking out in Ronald's massive land.

She saw the red barn in the distance and headed in that direction.

When she reached the arena near the barn, she saw a group of cowboys working their horses with roping calves.

She rested a foot on the bottom rung of the fence and watched.

She glanced down. Jack was sitting and watching intently.

Elana reached down to rub Jack between his ears. It was weird, he always made her feel better.

As if hearing her thoughts, he looked up at her and licked the back of her hand.

"Your dog looks like a cattle dog. Is he trained?"

She'd not heard the blond, blue-eyed cowboy approach her on a black horse.

She shook her head. "He's a rescue. I don't know if he was formally trained. But I've seen him herd a cow."

The cowboy tipped his hat. "My name is Lane Cooper."

She smiled. "Elana Taylor."

His eyebrows shot up. "Are you related to Cecilia Taylor?"

She blinked. "I'm her granddaughter. When did you meet Cecilia?"

A slow grin blossomed across his handsome face. "Mr. Ronald brought her over to meet us earlier."

She smirked. "And what kind of impression did she make on the cowboys?"

He laughed. "She'll keep Mr. Ronald on his toes."

A sudden wave of sadness washed over her. "I guess she'll be staying here, then."

Lane shrugged. "Seems that way. She said she is from South Carolina. Is that where you're from?"

She nodded.

He glanced over his shoulder. "Doesn't sound like you want to go back."

Elana sighed. "I have a job that I have to get back to."

He laughed. "Doesn't sound like you like your job very much."

She thought for a second. "I guess I don't. Maybe taking this road trip made me realize that."

He nodded. "So, get a job you like."

She cocked her head at him. "It's not that easy."

He rested an elbow on his saddle. "Isn't it? Life is too short to stay at a job you hate."

She studied him. "What did you do before you became a cowboy?"

He grinned. "I was an accountant. But I took a trip to

Montana for a month and realized I was a lot happier out here. So I quit my job and started working for Mr. Ronald. Now I make half of what I used to, but I'm twice as happy."

Elana pressed her lips together. "Was it scary? Starting over again?"

He gave her a reassuring smile. "Like you wouldn't believe. But it was also freeing."

The cowboys across the arena yelled at Lane to get his attention.

"I have to get back to work. It was nice meeting you, Elana." Lane tipped his hat to her before riding away.

"Start over," she murmured and glanced down at Jack. "Think I'm too old, Jack?"

Jack looked up at her and let out a bark.

She laughed. "I don't know if that was a yes or no. I guess I'm going to have to figure it out."

CHAPTER 37

*A*fter getting her emotions under control, Elana walked back toward the house.

Her father was standing on the porch glaring as she approached.

"Elana. I want you to know that if you don't get in there and get your grandmother to sign those papers, then I'm going to disinherit you."

She snorted. "Disinherit me? From what? Sounds like you don't have anything to give me, Father."

He narrowed his eyes on her. "I can have you fired from that job you love so much. Then where would you be?"

A range of emotions shot through her. Disbelief. Anger. Sadness.

She simply shrugged. "I guess that would make me free." She walked up the steps and brushed past him to the door. She reached for the handle and looked at him over her shoulder. "There's no need for you to reach out to me again after this. Not after I've seen your true colors. Goodbye, Father."

Elana opened the door and stepped inside with Jack at

her side. Closing the door behind her, she squeezed her eyes tight as a tear slid down her face.

After a few long seconds, she heard the SUV drive away.

"Elana, are you okay?" Ronald was at her side giving her arm a comforting squeeze.

She opened her eyes. Suddenly her grandmother was there pulling her into a tight hug.

She wasn't sure how long they stood there embracing each other. When they finally pulled away, her grandmother brushed her hair out of her eyes. "Come into the living room. I have something I need to tell you."

Elana followed Grandma Cecilia and sat beside her on the couch.

"I have decided to stay in Montana. Ronald asked me to marry him, and I said yes." Grandma Cecilia blushed.

Elana grinned. "I kind of figured that was going to happen."

She cocked her head at her. "So you won't try to talk me into going back to South Carolina?"

Elana slowly nodded. "You are an adult. You can run your business from anywhere. Although I hope you won't sign it over to Father. I think you need someone who will put the business ahead of their own selfless gain."

Grandma Cecilia nodded slowly. "I totally agree. That's why I want to sign over the business to you."

Elana gaped. "You what?"

Grandma Cecilia smiled like the Cheshire cat. "I want you to be CEO of the company."

Elana shook her head. "But I don't know one thing about running a business."

Her grandmother patted her hand. "I know, dear, but you are a quick learner. I'll help you with decisions."

Elana cringed. "But I don't even know if I want to go back

to South Carolina. I mean, I was starting to think about getting back into art."

Her grandmother nodded slowly. "I thought you might say that. Tell me, Elana, did you enjoy our journey here?"

Elana looked at her. "Some parts more than others."

Her grandmother cocked her head. "Where you would like to see yourself in six months?"

She sighed. "To be honest. I don't know. I've spent all my life doing what everyone has expected of me. Now, I'm not sure what I really want in life."

Her grandmother patted her hand. "Why don't you do this. You and Jack are free to stay here for as long as you like until you figure things out."

Elana smiled at her grandmother. "I think I need to find out on my own. I have some money saved up, and I was thinking I would like to take a trip of my own in the VW. Just me and Jack. You don't mind if I use the van, do you?"

Grandma Cecilia's eyes lit up. "I was hoping you'd say that. Before we left, I put the van in your name. She's all yours."

Elana blinked. "Are you serious?"

Her grandmother smirked. "You don't think an old lady like me is going to be traveling around in a van for the rest of my life, do you? I'm not crazy."

They all broke out into laughter.

"So, what will happen next?" Elana looked at her grandmother.

"Well, after the wedding, Ronald and I are going on a nice long honeymoon to Alaska." Grandma Cecilia grinned. "Don't worry about a thing. Once you get back from your journey, you can let me know what your final decision will be. Elana, I couldn't be prouder of you."

Elana looked at her grandmother. "Thank you. Without

you making me go on this trip, I would have been trapped under the thumb of my parents for the rest of my life." She reached for her grandmother's hand. "And thank you for teaching me that it's not impossible to start over in life. Life really is a journey that never ends."

EPILOGUE

*E*lana traveled around the States for close to six months with Jack at her side. She never thought she would be so happy under the blankets during a snowstorm with Jack to keep her safe and warm while snacking on Cheetos. She had stopped at a pawn shop in a small town and bought a cheap guitar. She would play songs to Jack while they sat around the campfire at night. At each stop, Elana made sure to capture the scenic view on her drawing pad. By the time she arrived back at Ronald and Grandma Cecilia's house in Montana, she had close to two hundred drawings.

Grandma Cecilia had informed her that her housekeeper in South Carolina, Anna, had taken Winston, her dog, and was enjoying helping to raise her grandchild. Anna promised to visit in the summer with her family.

Her grandmother also started wearing glasses. She told Elana that her doctor said she couldn't see squat, which would account for her mistaking a racoon for Winston that one time.

Her grandmother had also bought some property near

Billings where she was going to open a second manufacturing building for the company. She told Elana that that was why she had been sending her money to Montana. It wasn't being sent to Ronald. It was to establish a business banking account so she could open a second location.

Elana sat down with her grandmother, and they went over the ins and outs of business. Grandma Cecilia was pleasantly surprised at the innovative ideas Elana had for advancing the business. Elana finally relented and accepted the position of CEO if her grandmother agreed with new marketing ideas she had for the company. Grandma Cecilia agreed.

Her father tried fighting Grandma Cecilia in court. But he lost. Next came the foreclosure on the house along with losing his position at the company. Soon after, his wealthy friends disappeared from his life.

Her mother couldn't bear the shame and quietly divorced him. It seemed her father wasn't the only one hiding a secret. Her mother quickly moved in with a wealthy real estate agent in Florida.

Her sister Elizabeth rapidly distanced herself from their parents and moved to Charleston to start an interior decorating business. Brianna soon followed. and it seemed she soon became one of Charleston's top real estate agents.

To their credit, Elizabeth and Brianna, would contact Elana from time to time. Never did they ask for money. They also sent her a long letter asking for her to forgive them for how they had treated her over the years and hoping for some kind of reconciliation. Grandma Cecilia invited them for Christmas. Time would tell.

Elana didn't let the position of CEO rule her life. She still took long trips in the VW van with Jack and learned to let go of things she had no control over.

Most importantly, she was happy and at peace.

And if Jack could talk, he would say she no longer smelled like worry. She smelled like joy.

ABOUT THE AUTHOR

Jodi Allen Brice is an USA Today best-selling of over thirty novels. She writes women's fiction, small town romance, cozy mysteries, and Christian Fiction. Something for everyone!

You can find out more about her upcoming releases and appearances at jodiallenbrice.com

Join her newsletter for a FREE book!

The Mystery of the Drunkards Path
The Mystery of the Exploding Heart
The Mystery of the Log Cabin